Anne PERRY

A CHRISTMAS GATHERING

HEADLINE

First published in 2019 by
HEADLINE PUBLISHING GROUP

1

Cataloguing in Publication Data is available from the British Library

ISBN 978 1 4722 5717 8

Typeset in Times New Roman PS by Palimpsest Book Production
Limited, Falkirk, Stirlingshire

Printed and bound in Great Britain by Clays Ltd, Elcograf S.p.A.

MIX
Paper from
responsible sources
FSC® C104740

Headline's policy is to use papers that are natural, renewable and
recyclable products and made from wood grown in well-managed
forests and other controlled sources. The logging and manufacturing
processes are expected to conform to the environmental regulations
of the country of origin.

HEADLINE PUBLISHING GROUP
An Hachette UK Company
Carmelite House
50 Victoria Embankment
London EC4Y 0DZ

www.headline.co.uk
www.hachette.co.uk

A CHRISTMAS
GATHERING

By Anne Perry and available from Headline

Christmas Novellas

A Christmas Journey
A Christmas Visitor
A Christmas Guest
A Christmas Secret
A Christmas Beginning
A Christmas Grace
A Christmas Promise
A Christmas Odyssey
A Christmas Homecoming
A Christmas Garland
A Christmas Hope
A New York Christmas
A Christmas Escape
A Christmas Message
A Christmas Return
A Christmas Revelation
A Christmas Gathering

For a complete list of Anne Perry's Victorian mysteries,
including the Monk series and the Pitt series, as well as her
many other novels, visit:

www.headline.co.uk
www.anneperry.co.uk

To all who aspire to give mercy, and to receive it.

It was not the Christmas Vespasia had planned. Last year, in Jerusalem, had been unforgettable, filled with experiences that she could not even have imagined. They had changed her life, and her belief of heaven and hell. But this year, the second since she had remarried, she had hoped to spend Christmas entirely with her husband: no adventures, not even any parties. She had found, late in life, the man she truly loved with all the passion, intelligence and the trust in her nature. She had had her children and grandchildren, and had fulfilled all the obligations in society that she was heir to. This was different. In a purely personal way, it was her own time of fulfillment.

But as the carriage swept up the long curved driveway through the country estate of Max and Lady Amelia Cavendish, Vespasia knew from the look on

Narraway's lean, dark features that this was a duty he had steadied himself to face. His pleasure did not lie here any more than did hers.

They had discussed the visit only a little on the journey. It was to be a small gathering: old acquaintances spending Christmas together in the most charming surroundings. On the surface that was all it was. Beneath that, Victor would quietly, unnoticeably to anyone else, conduct some secret business. Until a short while ago he had been Head of Special Branch, that department under the aegis of the Home Office that dealt with anarchists, saboteurs and all purveyors of secret terror. Enemies were hidden, and success depended upon subterfuge, lies and misdirection. To Special Branch, success was when no disaster happened, indeed, when no one knew that there had ever been a threat.

The carriage came to a stop outside the magnificent façade of Cavendish Hall. A waiting footman opened the door and assisted Vespasia to alight, welcoming her by name. She thanked him and heard Victor's footsteps on the gravel as he came round from the other side, quietly thanking the coachman as he did so.

The high oak-panelled front door opened and Max Cavendish stood on the step, his handsome face wreathed in a smile. It was some time since Vespasia had seen him, but he had changed little. Rather more grey in his hair, perhaps, but otherwise the same. He inclined his head, not quite a bow. He would do that only for the Queen.

'Lady Vespasia, what a pleasure to see you. It has been far too long.' It was a polite remark without much meaning. Neither of them had been absent from society; they simply had few interests in common. She had even fewer with his wife, Lady Amelia, except social rank, and all the acquaintance and experience that that implied. Lady Amelia, like Vespasia, was the daughter of an earl; the title was her own, not her husband's, a fact that she never allowed him to forget.

Vespasia smiled with devastating charm. This must be played as if nothing but pleasure were in mind. 'I am sure this Christmas will make up for every year we have missed.'

He began to say something else, then changed his mind. She was not one to be flattered, as he had learned years ago. In her youth she had been considered one of the most beautiful women in Europe, not

3

just for her elegance of appearance, but far more than that: her wit, her grace and her bright courage to follow all her most passionate beliefs. As a young woman she had fought at the barricades in the revolutions that had set Europe afire with hope in 1848, now half a century ago! The darkness had closed over those hopes, but that passion had never left her. It was just that now, in her later years, it was a trifle more discreet.

'Delighted you could come, Lord Narraway.' Cavendish shook Victor's hand. 'I hope you had a pleasant journey?' He glanced at the sky. 'Weather's holding off, but I don't think it will last. Still … everyone's safely here. Do come in.' It was not necessary to add that the servants would follow with their luggage. As the century drew to a close, many things were changing in England – and everywhere else – but some courtesies remained.

They went inside to the huge oak-panelled hall with its marble-paved floor and sweeping curved staircases on either side, with polished banisters ending in high, elaborately carved newel posts. It was decorated with paintings of Cavendish ancestors of note for one thing or another. Frequently it was no more than the money to afford a fine artist, but no one would be tactless enough to say so. They dated from the time of Charles I right up to the present.

'Trilby will show you to your room,' Cavendish went on. 'Tea will be served in the blue drawing room at half-past four. But of course, if you prefer, you can have it brought to your room.'

'Not at all,' Narraway said immediately, for both of them. 'We will join everyone else.'

Such an answer, made without reference to her, confirmed Vespasia's feeling that there was much about this Christmas invitation that Victor had not told her. Twice she had drawn in breath to ask him, then could not find words that did not sound critical or demanding. She may not know his exact motive but she did trust him.

Cavendish Hall had at least fifteen bedrooms spread throughout the three main wings. Vespasia and Narraway were shown to one of the nicest, off the main landing and to the back of the house: quiet and overlooking the rose garden and the small lily pond with its central fountain. Vespasia could imagine the sound of it in the summer, with a light breeze and sunlight sparkling on the water. Now the garden was tidied and bare, preparing for a sleep under the snow that was forecast before the New Year. But they would be home again by then.

Their luggage followed them immediately, but of course the maid would unpack both their cases and put everything where it belonged.

'Are you coming down for tea?' Narraway asked, looking at Vespasia with some concern. It had been only a two-hour journey from London to this rural spot in the middle of Kent, but not one she was used to. 'Or we can …'

'Yes, of course I am,' she said with a smile. 'I will probably find I know several of the other guests.'

A shadow crossed his face. To most people he was unreadable, as he intended. He had had many skills in life, starting in the British Army in India, and then Cambridge University and law. He had crowned his career in Special Branch, climbing its ladder right to the top. He played by his own rules and had made both friends and enemies. He knew too much about almost everyone in government and society, and many outsiders too. Nobody doubted either his intelligence or his ability, but some were dubious about the core of his loyalties. Everyone had things he or she would very much prefer to keep private. Therefore, a man with so much knowledge was to be feared.

There was more silver in his dense black hair now; otherwise he had changed little over the years since Vespasia had first met him. He was still lean, not a lot taller than she, but she was tall for a woman. His eyes were coal black, the darkest she had ever seen in an Englishman, and there was both wit and strength in his face.

'I'm sure I'll find them interesting,' he said, referring back to the guests. He was equivocating, and they both knew that.

Would she ask him why? No. It was not the right time.

'I will be ready in five minutes,' she answered him.

She wondered again at his ulterior motive for accepting this invitation and, though she had managed a country house full of people for almost the whole of her life, she felt newly vulnerable because she cared so deeply to live up to Narraway's standards, as well as to her own.

Vespasia was wearing dark grey, with ivory lace, and of course pearls, when she entered the withdrawing room on Victor's arm. She heard the slight gasp of admiration, but she had been accustomed to that for

7

nearly half a century. Her hair was silver, her eyes silver-grey, her profile perfect, defying age.

Lady Amelia Cavendish detached herself from the guests with whom she had been in conversation, and came forward, a cool half-smile frozen on her face. 'My dear Vespasia! What a great pleasure. I'm so glad you were … able to come.' She emphasised the word 'able' as if Vespasia were lately disabled. 'We have all been looking forward to seeing you again.'

'Able, also willing,' Vespasia replied, hoping Amelia understood the implication that she might often have been able, but not willing.

Victor let out his breath slowly. He, at least, understood it.

'Let me introduce you.' Amelia turned towards the other people in the huge blue drawing room, with its windows on to the garden, dark velvet curtains sweeping from ceiling to floor. First, she indicated a man of average height, but made noticeable by his military stance and a certain confidence in his bearing. 'Rafe Allenby,' she said. 'And Mrs Allenby … Rosalind.'

'How nice to see you again, Mr Allenby, and to meet you, Mrs Allenby,' Vespasia said with a smile

8

she knew was charming, warm, and delivered with just the right degree of openness. 'As Lady Amelia says, it has been far too long.' Actually, she had known Rafe for many years, not well, but they had met briefly in exotic, Middle Eastern countries such as Lebanon, Persia and Egypt. Rosalind she had not previously met, but he had spoken of her with great respect.

A flicker of amusement crossed Allenby's face. 'How are you, Lady Vespasia? Indeed, it is. I have missed sharing your pleasure in so many things, and your stoicism in others. These days travelling lacks some of its old charm.'

Memories raced through Vespasia's mind: minarets outlined against the stars, the sound of camel bells in the night, a few mouthfuls of brackish water shared, laughter and aching muscles.

Allenby turned to Victor. 'Lord Narraway. I know you by repute, of course.'

Narraway smiled. 'And if you knew me better than that, you have more tact than to say so,' he said.

Allenby laughed. 'Indeed!' The remark clearly pleased him. 'Your reputation in Special Branch is—'

'Better forgotten,' Narraway replied.

'I am sure you are right,' Amelia said with a small

gesture of distaste, and a quick glance in Vespasia's direction. 'The very name "Special Branch" sounds like a pretentious name for something …' She searched for the right word. Clearly, she wanted one that was disparaging but could not find one sufficiently so.

Vespasia was aching to reply, but she was uncertain how much of the truth she should tell. It would look defensive … and yet the words slipped out. 'Socially, perhaps it does,' she said. 'Not professionally.'

Lady Amelia's eyebrows rose. 'Special Branch of what, for heaven's sake? Or is it tactless to ask?' Now there was definite distaste in her expression, as if it might be something faintly vulgar.

Vespasia longed to tell her that to need to ask was merely ignorant, but this was going too far. 'Not at all,' she said gently. 'Many sides of government are … not known to the general public.'

The colour rose up Amelia's cheeks. The idea that she was 'general public' was outrageous.

She lost her chance to reply as there was a young woman approaching them. Allenby turned towards her, his attention immediately held. She was unusual to look at, dark haired, dark eyed, but beyond her dramatic colouring she had within her a remarkable air of peace, as if there were something of great importance to her, of which she was absolutely certain.

'Iris, my dear,' Amelia said quickly. 'Come and meet Lady Vespasia Narraway. Vespasia, this is Iris Watson-Watt, and her husband.' She moved over to a young man with a very ordinary face, but well dressed and with a quiet, almost troubled air.

Vespasia felt instantly sorry for him, as if he had been left out of something.

'James Watson-Watt. How do you do, Lady Vespasia?' His voice was surprisingly deep and very pleasing. It changed his whole aspect.

As if she felt he needed some further explaining, Amelia added, 'James is in art ... somehow ...' She gave a slight shrug of her shoulders. She was becoming too thin, as was the fashion, but it gave her a certain elegance.

'Art restorer,' James explained. 'I can't paint, but I love to study other people's work. Brush strokes, use of colour and light, and which features they have chosen to accentuate.'

Vespasia suddenly saw him in a different way. 'What an interesting thing to do,' she exclaimed. 'I imagine you have developed many and varying ways

11

of seeing aspects of a painting. A face, for example? Or a hand?'

He smiled, and at that moment he was not ordinary at all. 'Exactly! A placement of light can change everything! A shadow or a plane highlighted can alter the whole mood of a picture, and one's perception of it. Take the bones around the eye, the angle of a cheek ...' He stopped and a faint colour came up his face. He had commandeered Vespasia's attention and he felt Amelia's gaze on him in disapproval.

'How kind of you to have invited such interesting people,' Vespasia said, turning to her, as if suddenly remembering she was still there.

Iris had an interesting face and Allenby's eyes were fixed on her, full of an emotion Vespasia could not read. She noticed that Narraway, too, was looking at Iris, but it was James's remark that stayed in her mind.

They were introduced to the last couple. Dorian Brent was in his late forties, or perhaps more. At the present, he looked tired and a little anxious. Vespasia's immediate thought was that he might have had a long journey to get here. He was standing next to his wife, who had a mass of heavily waving light auburn hair. It was extremely handsome, and only just beginning to lose the vibrancy of its colour. Her eyes were light blue, almost aquamarine, and her face had a fragile look, perfectly proportioned, and yet somehow brittle, an autumn tree with too many bronzed leaves on it. Her stature was unremarkable; colouring was everything.

'Georgiana Brent,' Amelia said, although she knew perfectly well that they were already acquainted, and had been for years. Her voice commanded Vespasia's attention and the momentary spell was broken.

'How are you, Mrs Brent?' Vespasia smiled at the woman, wishing to put her at ease. She seemed unnecessarily nervous.

'Very well, thank you, Lady Vespasia. And you?' Georgiana replied, giving a sudden smile. 'I can't think how long it is since we last met, though I remember the occasion.'

Vespasia was about to reply, but Amelia cut in. 'Lady Vespasia has lately retired somewhat from society. We are fortunate she was able to come here for Christmas.'

Again, Vespasia was stung. Amelia had made it sound as if she was too old to enjoy such events or even to participate. And the truth was that she had not wanted to come. It was solely Victor's wish, and her arguments had not dissuaded him.

She and Narraway had known each other for many years and had shared deep involvement in some of the darkest and most dangerous cases solved by Special Branch. Vespasia had been drawn in because of her profound friendship with Thomas Pitt and his wife, to whom Vespasia was related by marriage. Narraway had been Pitt's superior, and it was Pitt who had taken over the position of Head of Special Branch from which Narraway had been forced dramatically to resign. But the friendship between them had tested the limits of courage, and could not be broken.

Vespasia had realised only reluctantly that her feelings for Narraway were more than trust and a shared passion for causes, and a willingness to risk everything in pursuing them. He was markedly younger than she, and she had considered herself beyond his imagination as far as anything deeper or more intimate than friendship was concerned. She was still tasting such happiness with amazement. She had never cared earlier about reference to age: she had carried her years with grace. Her beauty had changed, but not dimmed. But since their marriage occasionally she felt absurdly vulnerable. She must conquer it.

The silence had been too long. She forced herself to smile at Amelia. 'Perhaps I was missing more than I realised,' she said graciously. 'I must remedy that. It looks as if this will be a remarkable Christmas.'

The situation was rescued by Max Cavendish rejoining them. Possibly he knew his wife better than she supposed. 'Narraway told me the other day that you spent last Christmas in Jerusalem,' he remarked to Vespasia. 'And had quite an adventure. The train broke down and you were kidnapped for ransom. He didn't tell me much more, but it sounds hair-raising.' He said it with a look on his face as if he envied them.

Vespasia remembered with a flash of total under-standing how utterly boring society could be, how meaningless the petty rivalries were in the sum of things that mattered. 'We must tell you more, at a better time,' she answered with a warmth that radiated through her. 'It made me see a lot of things in a totally different light. There are secrets, moments in life like that, but too few of them.'

'May I take that as a promise?' he asked.

'Of course.'

A uniformed maid with a white lace apron offered

to bring her tea, and Vespasia accepted. It was really very welcome.

Dinner was a less formal matter on the first night after everyone's arrival. Nevertheless, they were expected to dress specifically for it. The clothes in which one had travelled, whether by train or carriage, would not do for the sombre elegance of the dining room.

With only a few days left before Christmas, the house was already decorated for the season. Vespasia congratulated Amelia on it, although she knew the servants had actually hung the series of golden and silver bells, the wreaths of ivy and holly with scarlet berries, the perfectly tied crimson ribbons and bows, the lanterns and the mistletoe. They would have set and lit the moulded red candles, and the glass dishes filled with crystallised fruit, handmade chocolates and candied peel. There were even fresh roses from the hothouse, and wonderful shaggy golden late chrysanthemums on the side tables, and from Christmas Eve onwards there would be bowls of punch and, later, mulled wine.

The women seemed to favour red or green, traditional Christmas colours, for their evening dress, but Vespasia knew they did not suit her and chose instead a deep royal purple. She did not deliberately decide to be different; it simply happened that way.

She did not express any opinion at the table. She listened and observed. A couple of times she caught the eye of James Watson-Watt, and with complete understanding knew that he, too, was watching the other guests, including his wife, only he seemed also to be looking at the light, the richness of colours. His was not the only gaze turned towards Iris. Vespasia saw that Allenby's gaze turned to her more often than either to his wife or his hostess. So did Narraway's, but he was far more subtle about it. Perhaps only Vespasia noticed.

James also watched Georgiana Brent, and what he saw, despite her remarkable hair, seemed to disturb him. His face was more reflective of his feeling than possibly he was aware. Vespasia was sure that he did not like Amelia. He barely noticed Rosalind Allenby, except as good manners required when she spoke to him. He evidently liked her, but seemed not to find the light and shadows in her face interesting. It was a different way of regarding people, and Vespasia was drawn into it.

The meal was excellent, as she would have expected, but the celebrations were kept in store for

Christmas itself. She joined in conversation now and then, but mostly she was content to listen. Max Cavendish spoke about the trees on the estate, when they had been planted and by which generation. It was a heritage of beauty from the past, and to the future. He spoke of it with pride and gentleness. How many people round the table knew that it was only obliquely his, through marriage to Amelia, his second wife? Did anyone remember his first wife, Genevieve, who had died so tragically in childbirth? Vespasia had never asked about the child. It seemed too cruel a reminder of loss. It was forty years ago, at least. He seemed happy now, with Amelia, a distant relative of his, a Cavendish by birth as well as marriage. Vespasia was happy for him that he cared for the heritage so much.

She smiled at him as she caught his eye. She was surprised how much it seemed to please him.

Rafe Allenby talked of the political situation in the Middle East. He spoke of the present, but his vivid descriptions again carried Vespasia back to the past, and the occasional times their paths had crossed before. It had always been a pleasure. Had Rosalind Allenby any idea what a sensitive man her husband was, beneath the military exterior?

Their conversation moved on to various recent productions in the London theatre, and then at the appropriate moment, the ladies withdrew, leaving the gentlemen to pass the port around the table, and speak of weightier subjects, if they wanted. Max Cavendish did not indulge, but he always kept an excellent selection of cigars.

In the withdrawing room, the conversation was brittle. Traditionally, ladies did not speak of weighty matters, and that she was sorely tempted was not an excuse. Trivia bored her to distraction. Perhaps it did many women. And yet it could be useful. Sometimes you learned far more about another person from their unguarded chatter than you did from a serious and considered conversation.

Vespasia reminded herself of that as she took her part in the discussion of the latest news in society, moments both uncomfortable and shocking, and who wore what to which occasion, and how much professed horror was actually envy. She occasionally made people laugh, especially Iris, and that pleased her. The younger woman was very much an outsider to the group. Good manners kept her from inter-rupting, or asking to have references explained.

Finally, the gentlemen rejoined them, and within

a short time, one after another, each couple excused themselves and retired.

Narraway went up the stairs slowly, half a step behind Vespasia, and with his hand lightly on her waist. They had been married well over a year, coming towards two, but it still gave him intense pleasure to be able to touch her in such a possessive way, and have her lean towards him in response. He would immeasurably rather have stayed at home this Christmas and indulged in the small things that, in the end, were the most important: a poem shared, a picture in which they saw the same exquisite line, the same sunlight on the trunk of a tree, the same humour in a joke. He needed no one else.

But this visit was duty, and he had learned long ago that no happiness was untarnished for long if you had denied duty in order to take it. His mission was to take possession of some submarine blueprints, discreetly doctored, which were to be passed on through one of their usual networks in the hope that they would be accepted as genuine. These blueprints were changed so minutely that not even the expert eye would see the fatal flaws until too late. Even apparent allies could not complain that what they had stolen was not what they had expected. The unique amendments to these particular documents, however, would also lead Special Branch to the identity of a traitor in British Intelligence passing secrets to Germany.

But the visit here woke in Narraway old memories that were beneath the surface and, though healing over, were still painful. It had been a job like this one: a handing over of secret information, damning letters that would severely embarrass the Government. His role then had not been to handle the documents but to protect Edith, a young woman who worked with Special Branch and was entrusted with the transfer.

The occasion had been a summer house party in Normandy. Edith, with her extraordinary grace, her quick smile, was one of the guests. Narraway, unmarried, a little mysterious, quick witted, was another. The only one who mattered to them was Marie-Laure, who would take the documents to the next stage. She seemed so conventional at first glance, until one noticed her eyes, then her humour, then how she always seemed to be in control of the situation.

Of course, twenty years ago, no one knew that Narraway was even in Special Branch, much less how high his position. He had wondered since then how Marie-Laure was. He had even tried to find out, unsuccessfully. Perhaps her position was higher than he assumed.

Had he given himself away somehow? A careless word, an admission of knowing something he should not? Over the years, he had gone over and over every conversation, and could think of nothing. He remembered each scene, the grace of the château, the ancient stones it was built of, so mellowed with the land that he could not imagine the valley without it. He could see it if he closed his eyes: the clarity and freshness of the light, the flights of stone steps up to the terrace, the urns planted with flowers blooming extravagantly, spilling over the edges. The bright scarlet of geraniums and the unique smell of their leaves made him feel as if every other geranium must be a refugee, a copy of that garden.

He remembered coming up the walk and turning the corner on to the terrace, seeing Edith's body on the ground, skirt billowing on the stones, like a fallen flower, crushed. He remembered the disbelief, and the ice-like horror when he saw her face. She did not look hurt, or asleep; she had the emptiness of death.

He was numb with grief at first. Then a wave of failure overtook him. Everyone was appalled, or affected to be; all the house guests, those who were part of the plan one way or another, and those who were just there to make the party a genuine social event. They all seemed struck with grief – of course they did – whether they felt it or not. He could remember every nuance of it. The sober servants, even less obtrusive than usual, keeping their shock private. The sunlight shining on the old walls, the soft air blowing off the fields, smelling of grass and flowers. He could remember feeling almost motionless on the outside, the lazy summer wrapped around them, and yet inside he was furious, grieving, guilty, and all the time failing to find the answer. Or any justice.

He had finally left, as they all had, not knowing who had killed Edith. Of course, unlike all the others, except two, he knew why. Marie-Laure knew, of course, but Narraway only guessed the other: Philippe! On and off over the years he had thought he had a glimpse of proof at last, but it never materialised. The failure, the guilt were still there.

Of course, he had made enquiries through old friends, very discreetly, but he was certain there was more yet to find. There had to be something that would give him another clue.

So, it was necessary he do this one last favour for his contact in the Home Office, and take this packet of papers Iris Watson-Watt was carrying, and pass it on to his German contact. They would not believe in it from her, and it was vital that the German authorities were taken in by the misinformation they were to be given. Narraway's reputation, the disgrace in which he had left Special Branch, albeit totally false – and he had been exonerated – would still make the supposed treason he would appear to be carrying out believable. They must not suspect otherwise.

But he had not told Vespasia any details. He admitted to himself that this was, to some extent, not to spoil Christmas for her, but also maybe in even greater part because he still felt shamed by his original failure.

And how could he tell her without involving her, and thus endangering her?

They reached the top of the stairs and crossed the landing to their bedroom. At any other time, he would have appreciated its luxury, and its pride of place in the guest wing. That was a tribute to Vespasia, not to him. While she was born to aristocracy, he had only recently been elevated to the peerage because of his service to Her Majesty's Government. As Head of Special Branch, he knew too much about too many people to be liked. He was a private man; at the deepest level, a lonely one. Of course he had had affairs, but none that was lifelong, or gave him deep pleasure in the memory. Vespasia was the only woman he had truly loved, and considered his equal in both intellect and courage. But it was her wit and her compassion that touched him most deeply. In truth, he still found it hard to believe that she had agreed to marry him. It was like a crystal he barely dared touch in case he scarred some facet of it.

He wanted to give her his entire attention, but his mind was whirling with the possibilities of failure in this mission. Already he was wrong-footed by images, faces, and the burning deep memory of that other house party, years ago in Normandy. Of course, it was not the only failure, but it was the most profound. You could not deal with murder and treason and expect to be unscarred by the betrayal of those you trusted, the death of those you had cared for, and above all those who had lost their lives because of your decisions or your mistakes.

25

He thought he knew Edith's killer was Philippe, another of the guests – casual, charming, funny and cruel – but he was not certain, and from the darkness of memory the others at that house party all still mocked him. Was it injustice that galled him so much? Or pride?

And now he was repeating the situation with Iris. He was watching another young woman bring secret information, this time about submarine design, important for many reasons, and recently become more so. As naval power was shifting, becoming greater in Germany while Britain appeared to pay little attention, who gained supremacy under the sea would have mastery that could be decisive.

With it leading to the exposure of the traitor, this particular exchange was even more crucial. Iris had risked a great deal already bringing the blueprints up from a naval station on the south coast to give to Narraway. He must not fail this time.

He closed the bedroom door and temporarily shut out the world. Except that the barrier was imaginary. It would all be waiting tomorrow, and a night was a short time. He had to think, and plan. Passing things from one person to another was a part of his occupation. Doing it under the cover of a commonplace

26

social event was also quite ordinary. The enormity of this information, and the fact that no one must even suspect that it was uniquely false, made it far from usual. Had he lost his edge in the years he had been more or less absent? His insight, his cunning was what had made him top in his field. In a sense, his very aloneness had been an advantage, as well as his discomfort. Had ease of heart made him careless?

He looked at Vespasia unpinning her hair. As he stood watching, it fell in a silver sheet around her shoulders. He wanted to go across the room to her, touch her, feel the warmth of her skin, the ease of her response. It still thrilled him dangerously, with emotions he could barely control. It was far deeper than a mere physical hunger, it was a hunger for certainty of the heart, the ultimate safety. Was it too much to say it was safety of the soul?

But he could not concentrate. The sight of Iris had disturbed old memories, like a cave full of bats flying at him like ragged creatures with wings of splintered darkness. She looked so like Edith, whom he had been supposed to protect all those years ago. He had never known for certain who had killed her. He believed it was Philippe, a mysterious man about

27

whom the other guests apparently knew little, despite his seeming openness. But he never knew, could never prove it. It could also have been Jean-Claude, whom Narraway himself had caught out in a lie, or even the elegant host, Armand, who knew everything about everybody.

Was any of the other guests here to protect Iris? Allenby? Or Dorian Brent? Or Cavendish himself, as he had invited Narraway here? Narraway had not been told, presumably for extra security. But if Narraway could tell in these couple of hours, then the man was not much good at his job.

He should not let old ghosts throw his balance so thoroughly, yet only a fool does not learn from experience. Instinct was the subconscious mind putting together the odd facts your conscious mind has not realised form a pattern. It had saved his life more than once.

He had taken off his suit and hung it in the wardrobe, and was preparing for bed. Vespasia had gone into the bathroom. He had hardly said anything to her since they had left the withdrawing room. Some silences were utterly comfortable.

Vespasia returned and he took her place without a word. How could he explain any of this to her?

Half explanations, leaving gaps over what could not be said, were worse than silence. He would have to get the blueprints from Iris sometime in the next two days. Before Christmas, anyway. Did he imagine the tension in the air? Was it really only memory in his own mind, and guilt? He was angry. He looked down at his hand gripping his toothbrush as if it were a weapon and saw that his knuckles were white.

He looked at his face in the glass. Of course, it was older than in Normandy, much greyer, but had the same deep-set eyes, lean features, and brooding look, as if he were wanting to act dangerously, even violently. It was not an easy face, not comfortable. Why on earth had Vespasia chosen him? Could she possibly know how very much he cared? No one else imagined him having tenderness for anything, let alone vulnerability! They were afraid of him, of his insight, his ruthlessness, also his singlemindedness. He had let them think that of him. It was his best weapon. Many guilty men had secretly fallen apart because he looked at them a moment too long.

He dried his hands and put on his pyjamas. When he went back into the bedroom, only the night light was on. He did not disturb Vespasia, although he profoundly wanted to. He even hesitated in his step. The invitation to tenderness, intimacy was up to him, and he did not make it. His mind was too full of anxiety, fear, and yes, anger at old tragedies for him to have been gentle. That was a side of him he did not want her to know. Not ever.

He tried to blank his mind and fall asleep. He should do. It had been a long day, even though they had not travelled far. Vespasia had always found society easy. She was born to it, and her natural strengths were second nature. He was not born to it. Good manners, unforced and intelligent conversation were simple enough, but his background of the law and the army did not include women, except peripherally. His skills were learned and did not sit so easily.

But it was the wave of memory from the past that overwhelmed. Cavendish Hall was very different from that beautiful small château in Normandy. Now it was Christmas, not deep, warm summer in the French countryside, grasses up to your knees, whispering wind over the fields, huge, pale Charolais cows gently chewing in the sun. Here, there was the beautiful garden, the light on the stones, and the trees, and good food. But the purpose of the visit was the same, and the tension just beneath every surface conversation.

Here, however, there would be no death, just secrets, and a few people at least not meaning most of what they said.

He fell asleep at last, and dreamed of Normandy again. And quiet, graceful Edith, with the beautiful hands, and her body, lying motionless on the stones.

He woke several times, and went back to uneasy sleep, with variations of the same dreams. The path was sometimes different, but the end was always the same: confusion, and an overwhelming sense of loss. Then anger.

If he had been alone, he would have got up, paced to ease his restlessness. But he would disturb Vespasia, which would be selfish. Or more honestly, she would require an explanation, which he could not give. He had kept other things from her: things that were still secret, or things that had mattered at the time but were uninteresting now. The largest category was probably what had been necessary, but morally shadowed. Knowledge of events and facts he was unhappy concealing from her because they had been part of who he used to be, but a lie would have been worse. Once told, it was a stain, a darkness. And even the best explanations sounded like excuses.

He finally slept and woke only when Vespasia touched him gently and told him it was time for breakfast. She was already dressed in the soft shades of grey that suited her so well. And white, of course. White pearls, white lace at her throat.

He found himself smiling, shadows momentarily forgotten.

But at breakfast, the present imagery returned. Everyone else was at the table already. Graceful silver teapots and hot-water jugs rested on their own stands. Everything else was on the sideboard for the party to help themselves to: devilled kidneys, pork and apple sausages, bacon, poached or boiled eggs, fried potatoes, mushrooms. There were racks of fresh, crisp toast on the table, and of course butter and several types of marmalade. The dark, bitter Seville was always Narraway's favourite.

Greetings were made automatically, and enquiries after health. Narraway waited until Vespasia was seated next to Rafe Allenby, and then took the last empty place next to Georgiana Brent, who was not the companion he would have chosen.

Conversation was trivial. There was no news, either social or political, because there had been no newspapers delivered this far into the countryside. It was one of the profoundest of the many attractions of the place: so near London, and yet so far from its turmoil, either physical or intellectual.

They discussed travels of the past, and Narraway was content to listen and observe. People were often unaware how much their expressions gave away what their words did not. Dorian Brent was very interesting about his trips to Africa. His face became animated and he was probably unaware how often he used his hands to emphasise what he was saying.

Narraway saw how Georgiana watched him, but her eyes darted to left and right, observing the other women at the table, particularly Vespasia and Iris. They were both beautiful, each in her own way. Iris was young and had the flawless skin, soft hair, and perfect line of neck and throat that go with youth. She also had a grace that marked her apart from the others, and emotional intensity.

Or did Narraway imagine that, because he knew why she was here, the risks she had taken and would still take, to pass on this essential, dangerous information?

Vespasia was a classic beauty, and yet so much more than a perfect balance of feature and exquisite colouring. Age had diminished nothing in her wit, and intelligence had drawn the lines kindly. Self-mastery and a degree of defiance had kept her back ramrod straight and her chin high. He still looked at her with a thrill of pleasure, or perhaps that was what being in love was, that little surge of excitement that never died? And the protectiveness, the fact that she never bored him.

Allenby was talking to Iris's husband, James. Iris was listening. Both Max Cavendish and Dorian Brent were watching her. Were they aware of how intently?

Georgiana was. Narraway could feel her tension, as if she were touching him. Her body was stiff. She held her fork so tightly it looked like a weapon, and her actual food on the plate, the remnant of a sausage and a mushroom, had been untouched for minutes. Neither had she spoken, although he was aware that several times she had drawn in her breath as if to say something, then let it go again. Was she jealous of the younger woman, and of Brent's very obvious fascination with her? Was Brent the one who was supposed to be guarding her, as Narraway himself had failed to guard Edith?

Vespasia made polite conversation. Everyone was courteous, but no one really listened. She ate a lightly boiled egg and several slices of toast and marmalade. They discussed the weather and if it would turn colder. Would it be a white Christmas?

She wondered what had brought these disparate people together at this religious holiday, where the real meaning was honoured as much in the breach as the observance. It would never be that for her again, not after last Christmas in Jerusalem. One might tell others of the adventure, although she would have preferred not to. It had been part of the whole series of events that had changed her emotions for ever.

What were the Watson-Watts doing here? They were by far the youngest guests, by two decades at least. He was an artist, and not a wealthy man. The small signs were clear to those who knew them: ordinary shirts, good-quality shoes, but not new any more; an appreciative eye for other people's clothes, jewellery, a cigarette case, a tooled leather wallet, a silk cravat. But she thought it was for the quality, not the price.

Was he here because of Iris's position in society? He would not be the only man to attend high society events because of his wife. Indeed, Max Cavendish had done a lot of that earlier in his career. Vespasia knew that, although others might not. She pondered whether Lady Amelia had reminded him of it, perhaps more than once.

What had she expected? Looking across the table at her careful face and exquisitely coiffed hair, even at this hour of the morning, Vespasia wondered. She herself had merely piled hers up, but then hers was thick and heavy with natural waves. And she had always been beautiful. She knew all the arts, but seldom needed them. Perhaps she had taken too much for granted. That was a chill thought. She looked at Narraway, but as if following her earlier thought, his eyes were unmistakably on Iris. Was it by design that she wore that particularly rich shade, which one associated with the stately flower after which she was named?

As one grew older one remembered only the energy, the optimistic side of being young. Time removed many of the agonies of uncertainty, self-doubt, loneliness and the confusion that can hurt so much. Maybe it was just as well. Age brought its own difficult pains.

Georgiana Brent looked well this morning, but there was still that vague air of tension in her, a stiffness in her shoulders. Her bright hair was less jarring against the pale pink of her woollen dress. It was a fortunate choice. Vespasia would compliment her on it at an appropriate time.

Amelia offered to show Iris some painting or other, and Iris accepted. She had little gracious choice, and it would be at least as interesting as any conversation was likely to be.

Others declared duties or pleasures they intended to follow. Narraway excused himself, saying there were several books in the library he would like to look at. He smiled at Vespasia, but although he met her eyes, there was no communication in his glance. She felt almost dismissed. She knew that was foolish. Victor was here for some purpose. He knew she understood that.

'I shall take a walk in the gardens.' She rose from her chair gracefully. 'Even the little I have seen of them is inviting. And I doubt the weather will remain so pleasant for long.'

'Shall we have a white Christmas, do you suppose?' Rosalind said curiously.

'Hoarfrost, perhaps,' Max replied. 'That can actually be more delicate than snow, and I think more interesting. I'm sure you know what I mean, Lady Vespasia.'

'I do, and I should look forward to seeing it, too,' said Vespasia.

Amelia's eyebrows rose high on her forehead. 'Are you interested in hoarfrost, Lady Vespasia?' She sounded incredulous, as if it were some exotic and rather coarse taste.

'Yes,' Vespasia said immediately. 'I find it more sophisticated than mere snow!'

'How on earth did you know that, my dear?' Amelia said to Max. 'Or is it inappropriate to ask? I keep forgetting you knew Vespasia before I did.' She looked across at Vespasia. 'You have me by at least ten years.'

Iris drew in her breath sharply, plainly seeing the intended cruelty in the remark.

Vespasia hesitated only a moment. 'I have you by several things, my dear,' she replied, 'but it would be unkind to mention them. And unkindness is so unattractive, don't you agree? So revealing of vulnerability …'

Iris choked, but covered it quickly, her eyes wide.

Narraway looked startled, but he did not say anything.

Max groaned, just audibly.

'Yes,' Amelia said after a long moment. 'And it is so very ageing. But I am sure you have discovered that.'

Vespasia was prepared. She let her eyes travel very slowly up and down Amelia's face and décolletage. 'Oh, yes,' she agreed with a smile. Words were unnecessary. She flicked her skirt away from the chair and walked out of the room, head high, as if she were a queen, and she did not look back.

She heard a scuffle behind her, and a patter of feet almost running. As she was in the long hallway, she was aware of Iris catching up with her.

'That was exquisite,' Iris said with delight and respect. 'I am going to enjoy myself after all.'

Vespasia was amused, and felt a quick rush of sympathy. 'You have not been expecting to?' she asked with a smile.

Iris smiled back. 'Not a great deal,' she admitted. She began to add something, then it seemed discretion overcame her.

'Quite,' Vespasia said drily. 'I am not sure either …'

'But you are …' Iris began.

'The same age as the rest of the company?' Vespasia raised her eyebrows. 'No, I'm not. Amelia was right. I'm afraid I am rather older. And none of them would appreciate your suggestion that it is otherwise, even though from your point of view it may seem so.'

Iris looked momentarily embarrassed. Vespasia was instantly sorry. 'It comes down to what you remember,' she began to explain. 'Things that are history to you are memories to me. And I am afraid even Lady Amelia has far fewer memories than I have.'

Iris's face lit with keen amusement, very nearly laughter. 'However long she lives, I think that will always be true!'

Their glances met and they were both wise enough to say no more, at least on that subject. They walked on into the long gallery, and spoke of other things: art, philosophy, current affairs in other countries, even science.

A little later, Vespasia went to her bedroom to write a couple of letters to people she customarily contacted this time of year, and then brought them down to put on the silver tray in the hall ready for posting. She had not seen Victor since breakfast, but

she restrained herself from looking for him. He had
come here for some specific reason to do with his
previous profession and she would neither enquire
nor intrude. All his life he had taken a keen interest
in politics and secrets, both domestic and interna-
tional. His knowledge was probably greater than that
of any other man in England, and his skill beyond
measuring. He could not give it up easily, and
certainly not if his help were needed and asked for.

She had done her own fair share of discovering
and passing on secrets, even of solving crimes. Of
course, only as a most gifted amateur, with access
to areas of society all over Europe that few others
possessed. She understood. But she still felt an echo
of loneliness, even exclusion, that he had not allowed
her to share in this.

Was that what Rosalind felt? Had Vespasia's
sharing of memories of travels with Rafe made her
feel somehow excluded? As far as Vespasia knew,
Rosalind had never gone with him. A need, or a
preference, to be with her children? A dislike of
travel? Or perhaps she had not ever felt he wanted
her to be with him? Did she think or even know he
had secrets of some sort?

She understood that. She and Narraway had worked

together, but there had always been a separateness between them. She had been there because of Charlotte and Pitt, not because of Narraway.

Now she wondered what else she had not been as big a part of as she had supposed. She was aware of Victor's concentration on whatever this current matter was, and also that he was angry deep within himself about something to do with it. Some of his emotions were far more deeply cut off from her than usual. This was a pain he was not prepared to share with her, even by the acknowledgement that it existed. It was the first time since their marriage that she had been aware of it.

He was a deeply private man. She had always known that. She had first been married when she was in her very early twenties. There had been affection in the relationship, but not more. And then, long ago, affairs of deep passion. Victor had never married, until now. She did not ask about love affairs. She assumed them, and did not wish to know. There were questions one did not ask.

But perhaps Victor did not know that her marriage had been one of mutual respect and affection, trust in most things, but never that vulnerability that is inevitable in loving as deeply as she did now. She had not left herself those barriers of safety. Was that unwise? Or was it perhaps the ultimate courage? Was it wise never to care enough to be irrevocably hurt?

She told herself she was being ridiculous, of all the idiotic things, allowing Amelia's remarks about age to reach her. She would take a walk in the fresh air, as she had thought to do earlier, and think of other people rather than of herself. Amelia was unhappy, or she would not be so spiteful. Vespasia had assumed that Max was a very private man, kinder to Amelia when they were alone than he was in front of others. But perhaps she was wrong. Was his apparent strength of character merely the bullying of a weak man, rather than the protectiveness of one who cared? If so, Amelia could certainly use a friend. The woman's face reflected constant anxiety.

And what of the Brents? Was it Dorian's obsession, albeit discreet, with Iris that piqued Georgiana's jealousy? Or nothing to do with that at all? Maybe she was preoccupied with a family pressure or illness, or an illness of her own. One habitually talked politely, observed people's manner and dress, and knew so little.

Vespasia's mind returned to Rosalind Allenby. She

seemed almost … complacent. Was she oblivious of others? Had she not seen the gentleness in her husband's face as he looked at Iris? Was she used to it? Or did she not care? She would not be the only woman relieved if her husband's desires were elsewhere! Vespasia knew that painfully well with her brain, and yet if it were she, she could barely think of the wound. To imagine Victor was unhappy to touch her but was ever wishing to touch another woman was like a needle to the bone. Was Rafe Allenby's face reflecting anything more than lost youth, memories of dreams and imaginings long ago?

She collected her cloak and went downstairs and outside through the garden door next to the room where the flowers were arranged for the various vases throughout the house. It was not cold. She walked along the gravel path and then turned into the shrubbery. Further from the house, there was little wind; the huge cedars a hundred feet away protected that part of the garden from most of it. They stretched up and out in wide asymmetrical elegance. They had always been among her favourites, cedars and beech trees in full leaf in summer in the woods, or equally, the naked limbs of winter.

It was a huge garden, more than twenty acres, and old. The trees towered into the air. There was little flowering except a few shaggy chrysanthemums, and late crimson roses, and the last of the lilac and purple Michaelmas daisies, and the little winter Hellebore. It was far too early for snowdrops.

She moved almost silently, just a faint rustle now and then when her feet disturbed fallen leaves. That was how she heard the raised voices and came upon the two men without them being aware of her. They were standing in a small clearing, perhaps forty feet across, and with a small rustic seat near the centre. They were facing each other at about three or four paces, red-faced: young James Watson-Watt and the far older Dorian Brent. James was wearing a Harris tweed jacket, but Dorian had only the same woollen pullover he had worn at breakfast, as if he had followed James outside impulsively, rather than met him by chance. Neither of them was aware of Vespasia.

'Leave her alone!' James said angrily. 'For God's sake! You are twice her age.'

Dorian looked profoundly unhappy and awkward. 'I came out here on my own. You're behaving like a fool.'

'I wasn't saying you went with her,' James returned. 'You followed her! Don't bother to deny that, because I saw you!'

'I might have come out after her,' Dorian argued. 'I was not following her. I have no idea where she is. If you're afraid for her, then go and look for her instead of making a fool of yourself with me.'

'You followed her …'

'If you must know, I followed Allenby!' Dorian snapped. 'In case you didn't notice, he's been taking an unusual interest in her.'

'She's beautiful … more than beautiful.' The colour was rising even higher in James's face. 'She's … got a … magic to her …'

'Oh, for heaven's sake, get a grip on yourself, man!' Dorian was exasperated. 'She's an unusually pretty woman, and she has intelligence, although she is failing to use it at the moment. I came out to make sure she was all right …'

'That's my job!'

'Then do it!' Dorian shouted at him suddenly, and now there was fierce emotion in him too, arisen from nowhere and overtaking him. He flung his arm out in the furthest direction from him. 'Go and find her!'

46

James took a couple of steps towards him. Dorian must have misunderstood his intention. He lunged forward, swinging his fists.

James ducked sideways and lost his balance, only just regaining it in time to save himself from falling. He now completely lost his temper, righted himself, and came back with a sharp left jab. He did not look like a fighter, but he had excellent reflexes. He struck Dorian hard on the jaw, and he looked totally surprised. It was momentary.

Dorian struck back, landing a hard punch.

'Stop it!' Vespasia said loudly and very sharply. There was no mistaking that it was a command.

Neither of the men had seen her, and they stopped instantly, shaken with surprise more than anything else.

Vespasia walked very uprightly into the slight space between them. 'You are behaving like overtired children. I would be surprised if she had the slightest interest in either of you, at this moment.' She turned to James. 'Go and ask Cook for some ice to put on your face. If you don't reduce that swelling, you will have a hard time explaining yourself at dinner.' She dismissed him in a glance. 'And you, Mr Brent, should have grown out of such absurd antics long ago. No wonder your wife looks as if she's bitten into a bad egg, poor woman. If this is how you usually conduct yourself, I'm surprised she consented to come with you. You can both excuse yourselves from searching for Mrs Watson-Watt; I shall find her myself. Although she is probably back in the house having a hot cup of tea!'

'Lady Vespasia …' Dorian began, then looked at her face and changed his mind. 'I am concerned for her …'

'Nonsense!' Vespasia replied. 'You have been watching her ever since you arrived.'

'Lord Narraway—' he began, then bit the sentence off sharply. 'I assure you, I …'

'You have jam on your fingers!' she said sharply.

'What?'

'Like a child found in the pantry with jam on his face, and there's only one tart left on the plate.'

'You mean … oh … yes …' Dorian blushed. 'I was following her because I fear for her.'

It sounded perfectly ridiculous, but in spite of her better sense, Vespasia believed him. Most of what he said was absurd, and yet she was certain that some part of it was truth. She had yet to find out what it was, and she was reluctant to ask Narraway and force him to speak of whatever business he had here, if indeed it was even anything to do with that.

Vespasia was keen to prevent violence breaking out again. She turned to James. 'Go inside and straighten yourself up,' she told him. 'You look as if you have been dragged through a hedge backwards. I will look in the rest of the garden and see if I can find Iris.'

He hesitated. 'If you do, would you …?'

'Mind not telling her about this?' she enquired, her eyebrows raised. 'Of course, I shall not tell her!'

'Thank you…' James said awkwardly.

'But if you make a habit of it, she will certainly find out one day,' Vespasia pointed out.

'I won't,' he promised.

She smiled and walked past him under the trees again. At his age, she would not have known what jealousy was, or anxieties about no longer being the centre of someone else's life. She had been married to a pleasant, honourable man who did not feel the hungers and fears of great passion. That brought its own kind of pain, but it stirred only rarely now.

She had a good sense of direction and knew she was making her way back towards the house. It was a very pleasant walk. The garden varied considerably in its landscaping. It even included a good-sized decorative lake, with a graceful folly on the far side, white-pillared, very classical, like something that had strayed from a Greek sculpture. Very fashionable, a little while ago.

She came back towards the clipped hedges and more formal beds, soil freshly turned over, showing dark earth ready for spring planting. She had grown up in a country house with gardens like these.

She turned the corner at the end of the walkway and saw two people ahead of her. Even at this distance she recognised Narraway immediately. She always did. No one else stood exactly the same way, slender, immaculate, the light catching the silver in his hair. He was talking earnestly to his companion, his head bent a little towards her, as if what he said were intensely important. And she was also unique.

Vespasia froze. What on earth would she say to either of them?

Narraway put his hand on Iris's arm, gently. She was facing him, standing about a foot or two away. She laughed, and he held her arm a little more tightly.

Vespasia turned and retreated the way she had come. She did not look back at all, and went round the corner into the rhododendron walk, hardly aware of where she was. Perhaps James was not so absurd as he had seemed only a few minutes ago.

Narraway had tried a couple of times to speak alone with Iris, but each time he had been foiled by trivial circumstances. At least, he thought it was that. He had no way of knowing whom he could trust and whether these interruptions were by design. It was possible, of course, that Iris's protector also didn't know who to trust, and nor did Iris herself. Discretion was the only way forward.

The first occasion they had chanced to be alone in the long gallery, where the paintings were displayed that were of value, or of particular meaning to the Cavendish family. It was a uniquely pleasant room, lit well by natural light through a series of windows and glass doors that led into a paved area outside.

On the first occasion the previous evening, he had been looking at some of the family portraits going back to a more interesting period in art, and Iris came in alone, possibly to escape unwanted attention, or tedious polite chatter. But she was followed within a few minutes by Allenby, who looked annoyed at finding Narraway there.

The second time had been earlier today, when they had met in the garden room, on the way outside. This time he'd been interrupted by first a manservant collecting boots to be cleaned, and then by Dorian Brent, who had persisted in remaining with them, even though he must surely have been aware that he was intruding. Perhaps he did not care?

Or perhaps he was here to watch over her? The position Narraway had been in with Edith all those years ago. And failed so terribly. But how could Iris possibly pass him even the least bulky package of blueprints if they were never alone?

An ugly thought intruded into Narraway's mind. Could the failure all those years ago still be known? Was it a warning to the person delegated to guard a dangerous passing of papers of any sort, something that had to be physical, not merely a word or a message? Was Narraway a byword for failure, and he had just never realised it?

Now he was being absurd. He had been Head of Special Branch for years, one of the most successful chiefs they had ever had, and certainly the most feared. He knew too much, and not only knew it but understood it. It was both power and a vulnerability to know other people's secrets – another reason why he must succeed, and also a reason why he must not endanger Vespasia by telling her anything of his mission! At least until it was all over, when he had the package, had passed it on, and Iris was safe.

One of these men was supposed to guard Iris, as he had been supposed to guard Edith. Why the hell did they choose women so often? Because they were clever, discreet. One discounted them. In a way they were invisible. But, God, they were vulnerable!

Could they not have found a better way without involving a courier at all? He knew the answer before he had framed the question. They would not depart from the usual way because someone outside the system might be the one they were really looking for, and any change would alert them.

He was glad to be out of the whole deadly game of anarchists, spies, saboteurs and traitors, and yet part of him missed it. It was his skill. Apart from the episode in Normandy, he was good at it. How that failure still hurt! It was mainly the tragedy of the loss of Edith, but he had to admit it was also a wound to his self-worth. Vespasia believed in him, seemingly without shadow. What would she think of him if she knew of that? He admired her so profoundly, he needed her to admire him, too. Was that what he was worth? His mind, his knowledge, his courage, his unsurpassed abilities? Perhaps so. He had excelled, had been admired and feared for his skill. He had not family nobility, connections or wealth. Did that still matter? Was love such a fragile thing that image was more important than the intense, vulnerable reality?

He had barely spoken to Vespasia this morning. Conversation at breakfast had been general, but full of undercurrents. On the surface, still water, like a stagnant pond, but underneath, currents deep and surprisingly strong, a river with eddies unknown until it was too late.

He asked a footman if he had seen Vespasia.

'I believe she went for a walk in the garden, m'lord,' the footman replied. 'Up towards the beech avenue. If you take the path along the herbaceous border, you come out at the end of the trees.'

'Thank you.'

'But, sir …'

'Yes?'

'It's a very big garden, sir, about twenty-five acres.'

'Really!' Narraway said. 'I will try. Thank you.' He turned and went towards the garden door to take the man's directions. No use following after

Vespasia. He might try to meet up with her as she came back.

He was walking fairly briskly along the gravel path towards the clipped winter lawn on one side, and the dug over and cut down herbaceous border on the other. It was weeded and nearly bare, ready for the perennials to spring up again with the warmer earth, the bulbs to show, and in time the planting of new annuals. There was probably a head gardener, and two or three juniors to do the digging and bending, and of course regular removing of the weeds. They would restart at one end as soon as they had finished at the other. Hard work, and skilled, but creating beauty and harming no one.

He was thinking about that when he almost bumped into Iris, standing at the end of the path.

'I'm sorry,' he said. 'I was daydreaming ...'

She smiled. 'So was I. I'm glad we're here for Christmas. A garden like this is the right sort of thing to remind one of what matters. Don't you think?'

'Yes. And that we are entrusted with preserving it, tending it and ... protecting it,' he observed.

'Pulling the weeds?' Her expression was mildly amused, her eyes direct, quite undisguised by pretence, even of good manners. She knew he was the one to whom she had to give the package – of course, she had to know – but did she know who was there to protect her or had she information only on a need-to-know basis? He was chilled by another thought, as if a cold wind had arisen: he thought he knew what the package was, and its purpose to deceive a potential enemy, but also to trip the traitor who had given it, or who sold it to them. But why had he assumed he himself had been told the truth? All of it? How naïve of him. How arrogant to think he was above being used!

Iris was looking at him curiously. How much did she know, as opposed to thinking she knew? 'Where would be safest for you?' he asked. Let her choose.

She gave a twisted little smile. 'How about the orangery at midnight tonight? Or is that too obvious? Too early?'

'No, it's excellent. I shall have had enough dinner conversation long before that.'

'I have had enough already,' she said with a slight shrug. 'Lady Ammonia … Oh! Sorry. I said what I was thinking. I apologise. She isn't a cousin or something of yours, is she?'

'God, I hope not!' he said fervently. 'I think I can safely say that, other than my wife, I have no relatives in the aristocracy.'

'Lady Vespasia is quite different,' Iris said with feeling. 'As Lady Ammonia keeps saying, she is a lady by birth, not marriage. Lady Vespasia is a lady by nature.' She looked slightly surprised. 'And birth.'

'And marriage,' Narraway added with pleasure.

'Yes.' Her face shadowed. 'I must go, or James will think I am flirting with you. I'm sorry, I apologise for him. He is very sweet, really. He just has too much imagination. Most people have too little.' And with that throwaway remark, she turned and walked quite casually along the path and round the corner.

Narraway continued along his original path. He had no wish to meet anyone and be obliged to make conversation. It was a time and a day when he needed to think of the things that mattered. On this bleakly beautiful winter afternoon, when the trees were stripped of all their summer lushness that masked the bones, he saw a deeper loveliness, a truth of form. Winter, with its wind-torn clouds, its clean hard light, had always pleased him. The land was bleached of colour and, among the blacks and whites, the ploughed earth of the fields was accentuated in curves and folds.

Narraway had spent too long thinking about the

past. How foolish of him to allow those memories to take the present as well. And yet so many things reminded him of Normandy! Even though it had been summer then: deep, rich summer, ripe grasses waist-high in the fields, flowers tangled along the edges, as if someone's garden had over-spilled itself, huge pale cows grazing. Was there anything on earth more comfortable than sunshine, wind in the grass, and the sound of contented cows?

His rage was partly at the sacrilege of spoiling that.

He came to the end of the path and saw a flight of shallow paved steps, stone urns balanced on the pedestals at the bottom and top, empty of flowers now. The way the slanted light fell on them brought back memories of the château, Armand's château, with its balustrades and urns of flowers.

He was giving the past too much room in his mind. The present was beautiful. He had never been so happy in his life. He would tell Vespasia about Normandy when this current business was over. Or perhaps not. He would have to tell her why it mattered, why it hurt. She would think so much less of him, and he was not sure he could bear that.

He was allowing himself to appear different, and

that was a beginner's mistake! He increased his pace back towards the house and met Rafe Allenby on the lawn in front of the drawing-room windows.

'Lovely,' he said cheerfully. 'A marvellous garden. Could get lost in it with pleasure.'

Allenby smiled. 'One of the delights of visiting the rich. They do this sort of thing so well.'

'House parties?'

'Gardens,' Allenby corrected him. 'And Christmas, with a complete lack of responsibility. I love all my children.' A shadow crossed his face and vanished again. 'But not necessarily all my in-laws.'

'I haven't any,' Narraway replied, 'at least who visit.'

'Fortunate man,' Allenby said with feeling.

They walked in comfortable silence back towards the house, Narraway thinking his own thoughts, and presumably Allenby likewise.

Dinner was a very good meal, and everyone appeared to make the effort to be agreeable. Allenby in particular told interesting memories of his various travels, and even Georgiana Brent appeared to be engaged. For once, she looked at ease. She asked one or two perceptive questions, and Narraway caught a glimpse of a far more attractive woman than he had seen previously. The bitterness in her face vanished, as if it had been painted on the outside. Perhaps it was assumed only recently.

'Tell me more,' she said sincerely. 'We shall probably never go there, and even if we do, our pleasure will then be double.'

Allenby looked startled, and then pleased. 'My mind went to all sorts of things.' He continued. 'Camels have a strange lurching step, which appears awkward at first, then as you hear the camel bells in the darkness, and see their silhouettes against the paler night sky, lit with stars, you see the ineffable grace in them.'

'Ships of the desert, sailing through time ...' Vespasia murmured, but so softly only Narraway heard her. He instantly wondered if she had seen them with Rafe Allenby in the ruins of some ancient city, built in the dawn of time, when all stories were new.

'I thought of the old silk road,' Allenby went on, 'and wondered what precious things they had carried ...'

'Spices?' Cavendish suggested.

'Jade?' Amelia said as an addition. 'Polished, carved, made into marvellous shapes. And ivory, of course.'

'Fur?' Iris asked.

Amelia raised her eyebrows. 'From China? Hardly, my dear.'

'Wouldn't the trading posts along the Silk Road have treasures from the north as well?' Dorian asked. 'Furs among them?'

'And walrus ivory, for example?' Vespasia added.

'Anyone would think you'd been along it!' Amelia stared at Vespasia, her lips twisted an amusement.

'Only as far as Samarkand,' Vespasia smiled sweetly. 'But I have heard some wonderful tales by firelight, under the stars.'

'And told a few, I imagine,' Amelia said instantly.

Vespasia's smile remained exactly the same. 'Only imaginary ones,' she agreed. 'I keep the true ones to myself.'

'Less interesting, no doubt,' Amelia nodded, as if in agreement.

'Less unkind to others,' Vespasia corrected her. 'And less likely to be repeated with malice and error.'

Amelia started to respond, then realised she had no answer and remained silent.

Surprisingly, it was Georgiana who rescued the conversation. She turned to Narraway with interest. 'I believe you spent time in the Indian Army, when you were very young. Or have I been listening to the wrong gossip?'

'No, you are quite right,' he assured her.

'Many memories?' she asked.

His mind teemed with them. 'Good and bad. But it was an experience I would not have forgone.'

'You are fortunate,' she said quietly. 'I had many I would forgo gladly. But even if the mind forgets for a while, the bones remember.' She did not explain her remark.

Narraway looked at her with more interest than before. He wondered what, in particular, she was referring to. He knew almost nothing about her. That was an omission he should not have made. He did not yet know whether Dorian Brent was the person who was here to assure Iris's safety, and since Georgiana was Dorian's wife, he should have got to know her better, because he should have known all of them. At first he had imagined it was Cavendish, and that was why they were at Cavendish Hall. Vespasia knew Amelia Cavendish, and knew Rosalind Brent a little, at least by repute, but it would be rash to make assumptions about any of them.

Georgiana was staring at him, eyes wide.

'Yes,' he agreed. He was thinking of Normandy

when he spoke, but the same truth applied. 'The bones do, like an old injury that seems healed, but aches when the weather takes a certain turn.'

Her face was tense with recognition of tragedy. 'Were you there for the Mutiny? That must have been about then. Or are you too young for that?'

'I was young,' he said bleakly, memory flooding back. 'Not yet twenty, and very green. But I remember the aftermath particularly. Not something I wish to relive in my mind ... ever.' He had not meant to embarrass her, but the memory of brutal violence was one of the worst in his recollection.

'I'm sorry,' Georgiana replied softly. 'Of course not. I did not see that, but there are other things. No two people are the same. And there can be deep wounds, even in calm countryside like this. Violence does not always come screaming, and with a bloody sword in its hand. It can come wearing a familiar face, and armed only with words ...'

'What a harsh subject for Christmas,' Rosalind said with forced cheer. 'It's a time for forgetting old injuries.'

Narraway thought briefly of a governess he had known long ago. She smiled just like that when announcing it was time for rice pudding, or bed.

But it was Vespasia who spoke. 'No, it is the time for forgiving them. That way, they stay buried, instead of rising like malevolent ghosts every time there is a tear in the fabric.'

Narraway glanced at her, and then away again. He knew just what she meant, and there were tears in the fabric greater than he had thought.

The conversation washed over him: more talk of where people had been, the marvellous and the strange things that they had seen, the interesting people, food, the humour, and the commonality of laughter, and the love of children, and making something beautiful. But he was not listening. Actually, he was watching their faces. Faces gave away far more than many people realised. What made different people laugh? Particularly, what remained in the memory? Necks and shoulders, especially of women, in soft lines, and the fabrics of dinner dresses. Even the colours they wore, not necessarily to flatter, or even for fashion's sake; sometimes the colours were statements of their own natures. Vespasia so often chose greys, blues, or the palest of sand, ivory, or oyster. She loved the delicacy and the suggestion of mystery in the colours of the sky and the sea. Otherwise it was lavenders or purples. Ancient royal colours, vivid or subdued, half shades. Would he even recognise her in red?

Lady Amelia wore plum, a rich, subtle silk. Clever, with her cold colouring, and individual.

Rosalind chose comfortable blues and browns, nothing challenging. Narraway thought it was in order to appear that way. Travel the world all you wish, but this is the comfort you come back to!

Iris chose purplish blue, simple in line. The gown was the setting, as one frames a painting not to detract from it.

Georgiana wore burning orange and gold, mirroring the exact shades of her hair, but brighter. It was certainly spectacular. Whether it was flattering was another matter

Lastly, he turned back to Vespasia. She had delicate bones, yet there was startling strength in her face.

She turned to him, as if aware of his gaze, and he looked away immediately in case she saw his emotion too naked. At times, it was painful to be so much in love, and at his age perhaps people would think it ridiculous. She had known him only a few years, and there were other things, darker, that she did not know of and might find very difficult to understand, let alone forgive. Certain espionage was not a clean-cut thing.

She had never asked. Did she have enough wisdom to know she might not be able to live with the answers? How much longer did they have together? He had no idea. Whatever it was, it was not long enough. If you are happy, it can never be long enough.

Everyone was agreeable to going to bed early. It had been hard to find conversation after dinner. No one wanted to sit late trying to make any further effort.

As soon as the bedroom door was closed, Vespasia faced the issue. She stood in the middle of the floor, looking at Narraway. She had considered many ways of approaching this. None of them pleased her, but that was an excuse, and she acknowledged it to herself. 'What is the matter, Victor? Do you know something about one of these people that you would rather not?'

He looked startled. He shouldn't be. She had tried to approach the subject several times and he had closed it. Cleverly, it was not obvious, but she knew him, at least in some ways, perhaps better than he had realised.

'Very little,' he said with a brief smile, there and then gone again. 'In fact, I know nothing that isn't general knowledge to everyone. Of course, I don't know society nearly as well as you do.'

'None of them is my friend; they are only acquaintances, and that means little. It's the surface, not the reality.'

'Knowing about people is often a damned good reason not to be friends,' he said drily, walking across the floor and past her towards the wardrobe where he could hang his dinner suit when he took it off.

It was easier, and yet it felt a kind of closure, almost a denial. He did not touch her as he passed, not even the light brush of his hand on her shoulder.

'You're not friends with Amelia, yet it is plain you both know more about each other than the rest of us do.' He took off his jacket and put it on the clothes hanger.

'Superficial,' she said briefly.

He glanced at her. 'The information may be superficial, but the understanding of it is profound. You dislike her as much as she dislikes you, but the reasons are different, and in your case, it is not rooted in jealously.'

So, he'd been watching her! And Amelia. Habit? 'And you think that in her it is?'

He looked up at the ceiling, and then down again,

a roll of the eyes, not of the head. He turned away and took off his trousers to hang them up. They must be immaculate for tomorrow evening. Cavendish Hall servants would launder all shirts and personal linens.

'Not over Max, I assure you.' She forced herself to sound amused, rather than hurt, that he was giving her only half his attention. And yet she had deliberately kept her hurt out of her voice. It was beneath their relationship to use emotional pressure.

'Of course not,' he agreed, still with his back to her as he hung his trousers. 'He is far too self-satisfied for your taste. His involvement is towards an end. I don't think he does anything for its own sake, because it is fun or beautiful or interesting, except as it affects something further.'

For an instant she remembered standing beside Victor and watching the wheel of the stars making their slow progress across the summer sky, and marvelling at the endless universe. It was an activity where the sole purpose was the thrill of such awe. That was when she felt the prickle of tears, which was ridiculous. How could you feel so alone when someone you loved intensely was standing eight feet away?

'You read him very well. But he is not the only self-absorbed and empty man.' She unfastened her dress, taking it off carefully. It was one of his pleasures to do so, but apparently not tonight, and she certainly would not ask. It was not pride; it was so as not to spoil the pleasure of his doing so when it happened again.

She took the pins out of her hair and let it fall around her shoulders. She brushed it without looking at her reflection, and tied it in a loose knot where it would stay untangled through sleep. He could pull the knot out easily enough, if he chose.

He did not choose. They went to bed without further meaningful conversation.

She lay on her side, facing away from him. He was not open to speech, let alone touch. It seemed like a long time before she finally fell asleep.

She woke sometime in the night and was aware of an empty bed beside her. Presumably, he had gone to the bathroom. It must have been his movement that had woken her. She would pretend to be asleep. It was not the sort of thing on which one commented.

Half an hour later he had not returned. Now she was worried. Was he ill? She turned up the gas lamp beside her bed and got up. There was no light anywhere else. The bathroom was empty. Victor was not anywhere in their rooms.

She returned to bed, turned out the light, and pulled the sheets up to her chin, but she could not go to sleep.

Narraway had not been able to sleep either. He had known he must get up again, silently, in three-quarters of an hour, dress, and find his way without turning up the gas anywhere, and get to the orangery by midnight. He had not woken Vespasia. He would tell her about this when it was over. At least, about part of it. Better to leave Normandy out of the account. All he could do was prove that his past mistake was not part of a pattern.

At quarter to midnight he had slid silently out of the bed he would so much rather have stayed in. He had tiptoed over to the cupboard, collected his clothes, and had gone to the bathroom and dressed.

He had closed the outer door softly whilst Vespasia was still sleeping. There had been two gas brackets burning on the huge landing and down the stairs. He had been able to see quite clearly to make his way down, across the hall, and along the passage that ultimately led to the conservatory and, beyond that, the orangery. He had worn soft rubber-soled shoes so that he could move soundlessly.

* * *

It was further than he had thought, and of course the dimmest of light he moved more slowly than when he was here in the daylight. He passed the entrance to the long glass-paned conservatory, mostly for flowers. The orangery was next. It was a very large space, for a private house, at least forty feet by about fifty, and the orange and lemon trees were old and reached almost to the arched glass roof. One could hide half an army here ... in the dark.

He opened the door, slipped in, and closed it behind him.

The smell of damp earth and leaves was rich, but at this time of the year, even though orange trees held blossoms, buds and fruit all at the same time, there was little of the last. As his eyes grew accustomed to the complete darkness, except from the little starlight that came through the glass, he began to walk forward round the trees, looking for Iris.

He heard the door latch, just the faintest snick. He turned and crept back. Then he saw her, motionless, listening. Her silhouette was unmistakable. No one else had that profile or held her head in just such a way. 'Iris,' he whispered.

She heard him immediately and turned. 'Lord Narraway ...?'

71

'Here. Come over here.' Better they both stand in the shadows. Habit. Who else would be up at this hour? Did you ever grow too old for assignations?

She was beside him already. He could feel a small package wrapped in oiled silk being put into his hand. It was not as large as he had expected.

'Thank you,' he said softly. 'Now go back to bed and pretend nothing happened. But … be careful.'

'I will.' She reached up and touched his cheek with one finger. Then before he could add anything more, she had melted into the shadows and all he was aware of was the faint sound of the door closing, and then the smell of the earth and the orange trees again.

He moved away from the trunk out on to the side of the path, then back towards the door. He was about to open it when he felt, rather than saw, movement to his right. It was so slight, he was not certain if he had imagined it. But there was no wind in here. After a few moments, there was a feeling of almost no air.

He waited. Nothing else moved, but he had the almost certainty that there was someone else in this huge room with its trees. There was another door. It was to the outside, but he would go through it, along the outer walk, and return through the garden room. That lock would be easy enough to pick, if he had to.

He moved one foot, then the other. A branch slightly over his head brushed leaf on leaf. Had his head done that? Or someone else. What were they there for? An assignation? Two, in the orangery, in one night? There were only ten of them in this huge house. And all of the servants, of course. Would a servant use this place for meeting? Why not? He or she would hardly expect anyone else to be here!

He walked soundlessly across the aisle and into the deep shadow of another tree. And then another. He was yards from the further door. He could see it. The big bolts would make a noise. Whoever it was, the other person would both hear him and see him. But it would be quick. Once outside, he could sprint to the nearest trees, about fifty feet, if he remembered correctly.

Or he could simply come out into the open and go through of the door directly into the house, the way he had come. But how would he explain himself? What explanation was there that would not be both ridiculous and grubby? Every man would suspect his wife, unjustly. Unless, of course, they thought it was one of the maids? And that would be even more unjust. Vespasia might believe the truth, but she could not prove it to anyone. She would be very publicly humiliated. He felt sick at the thought. There were things he could not lose: her trust, her love. No use trying to shield himself from the pain, even in the imagination. He loved her more than he knew how to deal with.

Silently, he went over to the door, drew the latch sharply, yanked the door and went out, the same moment that the bullet slammed into the frame.

He threw himself across the pathway on to the grass and rolled over, at least out of the direct line of fire, then scrambled to his feet and ran for the nearest bushes. By now his eyes were used to the dark so he could see their denser outline against the background.

Quickly he crouched behind them and then looked back towards the house. He could see the dome-shaped roof of the orangery quite clearly, and the starlight gleaming on the glass roofs of the orangery and the conservatory. He searched for the door he had come out of, and saw it clearly as the light caught it in movement, and then was gone. Somebody had closed it, but from the inside or the outside? He strained his eyes but could not see any figure, or any more movement at all. Did that mean someone had shot at an intruder, and then, not seeing him when he opened the door, gone back inside and locked it?

Who? A night-prowling footman with a gun?

Hunting what? A poacher? In the orangery? That hardly made sense. Why would a footman be armed, for heaven's sake? To shoot an indiscreet guest keeping a tryst with someone? That was absurd.

Outside, it could have been a gamekeeper, except there was nothing in the formal gardens to poach. Pheasants, rabbits, or anything else would be in the woodlands beyond, acres of them!

He could not stay here all night. Apart from anything else, it was perishing cold. After the shelter and artificial warmth of the orangery, he was even more aware of it. He was forced to the last explanation, the one he had been avoiding. It was to do with the package Iris had given him.

Narraway stood up very slowly until he could see the path curving towards the garden door, and realised just how far he had to go, and in which direction.

Another shot rang out and he heard it whistle past him and tear into the branches of a low tree behind him, striking the trunk. He dropped to the ground, his breath tight in his chest. It had not come from the same direction, not quite. Whoever it was, they were outside! And coming towards him!

He ran, bent double, moving as fast as he could. With the earth as bare as it was, there was little foliage to hide behind, only stalks, mounds of roots and tubers, and bare, smooth, well-dug dark earth that clung to his feet.

Where was there a holly bush, or a laurel, things that keep their leaves year round? He tried to peer through the darkness and to remember what he had seen when he walked here this morning. That seemed an age ago now.

He should not remain here any longer. If only the other man would move again. Narraway could see nothing, no matter how he strained his eyes. He had to cross about ten yards of the lawn, whichever way he went. There was no cover at all. Run, swerve, keep going as fast as you could.

Even as he thought this another shot rang out! Closer to him this time. Who the devil was it, and why? Did someone think he was a burglar? Nice thought. Far too comfortable. The first shot had come from inside the orangery. Thank God Iris had already gone. But the only answer that made complete sense was the worst one: the person firing was one of the guests in the house, or the host. Face it.

Narraway picked up a clump of earth and threw

it about a dozen feet away. The answering shot was unmistakable and closer.

He got to his feet and, bending low, ran towards the only holly tree whose position he could remember. He ran, zig-zagged, and twice rolled over a little sideways toward his direction of travel. There was one more shot. He thought that was six altogether. A pistol? Probably. Not a rifle. Certainly not a shot gun.

How was he going to get back into the house if he had to pick a lock, which he could do only standing in front of it where he would be a sitting duck? And no one would hesitate to blame the shooter. What the hell he would say he was doing? If he was alive to say anything?

But then what was one of the guests doing, walking around the house at night with a pistol, taking shots at an unknown figure? There was no good answer. He had a bitter enemy in Cavendish Hall who was just as prepared to take risks as he was. What excuse would they use? That he thought Narraway was a burglar breaking in?

If he could get close enough to a door to be recognisable, he might be safe.

Now only ten feet to go. Several minutes since the last shot. Was the assailant still there? How long should Narraway wait, shivering more and more with the cold, now that he was not moving?

He decided to go a little further round, so he could say he had come out through another door and accidentally locked himself out.

He went twenty yards, around an angle and then along the main façade of the back of the house. Then he straightened up, muscles clenched tight with fear and cold, and walked across the open gravel towards the garden-room door. He put his hand out, wondering second by second when he would hear the shot a half-instant before he felt the impact of it tearing through his flesh.

The handle moved. Round … all the way round. The latch clicked and the door swung open. He pulled it wide and stepped in. His hands were shaking as he closed it behind him and felt his way through the room carefully, and on into the corridor beyond. Here it was lit by gas lamps flickering on the walls, spreading only a few yards of glimmering light.

He walked quickly across the expanse of the hall, glancing behind him more than once, to the bottom of the stairs. He saw no one. At the top, he turned towards his own bedroom … his and Vespasia's. If she was awake and had heard the shots, or his movement woke her, what was he going to say? Maybe nothing, but not a lie. Definitely not a lie.

He turned the handle and pushed, then he let out his breath. The room was in darkness. Thank God! He went in and closed the door behind him. He was soaked in sweat. His clothes stuck to his body. He should take a bath, to get clean and warm. But that would waken Vespasia and he would have to explain, or try to.

Instead, he undressed, leaving the package in his jacket when he hung it up, donned his pyjamas again, and very carefully got back into bed. He could feel the warmth of Vespasia's body. He ached to be able to hold her, let the ease soften the pain inside him. But that would be selfish. He might have disregarded that, but not the necessity of explaining why he was freezing cold, still shivering not from the wind in the night, but from the fear of being shot at, and knowing that the life that had become so precious to him could be snatched from him in an instant … just a bullet an inch to one side or another.

It was a long time before he finally fell asleep.

He woke heavy-headed and still aching from the chill of the night, and the tension his body would not let go of. But he worked through it, dressing quickly, shaving and trying to make himself look a little less as if he were coming down with a chill. He was not yet prepared to explain anything to Vespasia.

He asked her to go down and begin breakfast, and he would follow her in a few minutes. As soon as she was gone, he went to the jacket he had worn last night and took the package out of the inside pocket. It was almost three or four inches long, eight inches across and half an inch thick. The altered submarine blueprints.

Competition to develop subaquatic machines was razor sharp, progressing week by week. The Swedes were brilliant; the Americans had been among the earliest. And apparently Peru excelled, too. Britain was a little late on the scene, but they had now made up for it by a recent speed in development … so one believed. Hoped! This package, destined for Germany, represented only minor new details, but critical. They were very slightly falsified: just a figure changed, a proportion. But it would be sufficient to make the whole thing useless, and perhaps take months, even years to find and correct. But perhaps even more importantly, it would enable British Intelligence to catch the traitor in their midst.

Where should he put it? There were two possibilities: put it where it was invisible to the casual eye, even to the informed search, or leave it where it was, in the open, but appearing to be something else. He favoured the latter because it had a far better chance of success. Any competent person could pick the lock of a case or cupboard. The outside door would not even be locked. Who locks a bedroom door from the outside in a private house?

How to disguise it? Anyone searching for it would look through all his possessions, and the room itself. There were very few hiding places. The answer was obvious: he must hide it among Vespasia's personal belongings. She had not much jewellery with her, but small things to do with her toiletry, underwear, and so on. And he must make the initial decision in the next few minutes ... five at the outside.

He opened the drawer of her handkerchiefs, long white gloves for evening wear, silk or lace scarves or fichus, and below them, other silks. He picked out a place and slipped the package in. He would have to tell her, of course, but later. Now he must go down to breakfast, before she came up to see if he was all right.

He joined the company at table and noticed

immediately that he was not the only one to be late. Neither Iris nor James Watson-Watt was there. Had they slept in? It would be clumsy to ask, and possibly tactless.

He wished everyone good morning, then helped himself from the sideboard and sat down. A chair had been left vacant for him beside Vespasia.

Conversation resumed. He ate rather than join in. It was strange to glance around the faces and realise that almost certainly one of these people had shot at him during the night. Since the shooting had begun in the orangery, the assailant seemed unlikely to be an intruder. It could, of course, be a servant, but that also seemed unlikely, given that a servant would not so easily ascertain Iris or Narraway's movements. Cavendish? Dorian Brent? Allenby? James was an unlikely suspect, unless he'd acted out of some crazed jealously that meant he was completely unhinged. And he did not look so. Had he any idea that his wife worked for a secret department of the Government? Was Narraway ruling him out only because he seemed so innocent? That would be unwise. He knew better than that.

James himself broke that reflection by appearing in the dining room looking dishevelled and distressed.

His face was flushed and his thick hair untidy. 'I can't find Iris,' he said before anyone could ask him. 'I've looked everywhere I can think of.'

Amelia was startled, but then she composed herself immediately. 'Could she have gone for a morning walk in the garden?' she said soothingly. 'It is very pleasant, if a little cold.'

'For this long?' he said desperately. 'I've been looking for her … perhaps it is not as long as I think …' He looked confused, desperate.

'It is cold,' Vespasia agreed. 'Have you looked to see if her coat is missing?'

James steadied himself a little. 'Her shoes,' he replied. 'Her outdoor shoes are still in the cupboard.'

Narraway felt the cold touch him, not on the outside of his skin, but deep inside him. He put down his fork and stood up. 'I'll come and help you look.'

Vespasia pushed her chair back and stood also. 'I'll come too, just in case she is not well … or is in any distress.' She took Narraway's arm.

Actually, he was glad of that because he was suddenly afraid. He had heard Iris leave the orangery, but where had she gone?

Narraway and Vespasia left the room and no one made any attempt to stop them, although there were murmurs of awkwardness and trying to soothe away unnecessary concerns.

As soon as they were beyond the dining room, Vespasia turned to James. 'Where have you looked, precisely? The servants' quarters? Whom have you asked?'

James made a visible attempt to control himself. He looked very young and fearfully vulnerable. 'I asked the chambermaid, one of the footmen, Mr Cavendish's valet, whom I passed in the corridor, and the tweeny maid I met on the stairs,' he replied.

'That seems very thorough,' Vespasia agreed. 'But her outside shoes are still in the wardrobe?'

'Yes …'

'The conservatory?' Vespasia suggested. 'It is very pleasant there, and dry underfoot …'

'For an hour?' James's voice rose in pitch and his panic was only too clear. 'I've looked for her for an hour.'

Narraway's first thought was that James did know the work she did, and that was why he was so afraid. 'The orangery,' he said. 'I'll go and look there …' He turned and walked away without explaining why he had made the suggestion. He had heard Iris leave last night, but could she have gone back? Why? But it was the one place he could think of that James had not mentioned.

With barely a moment's hesitation, Vespasia and James were on his heels. It was a long walk, first to the conservatory, and then to the far end of it, into the wider, higher orangery, a luxury few houses had.

He threw the door open and stepped in, the now-familiar smell engulfing him, and with it the sharp remembrance of last night. He looked around.

'Oh! Oh, dear ...' Vespasia did not scream – she never did, whatever the circumstances – but the distress was sharp in her voice. She moved forward and bent down, and that was when Narraway saw the white foot under the branches of one of the larger orange trees.

For a moment, he could barely draw in his breath. Then he went to Vespasia's side, kneeled also, and drew the heavy, low-hanging branches aside. Iris was lying half on her back, two scarlet welts across her bare shoulders, one extending to her neck. Her eyes were closed and he could see no movement at all. He felt his own breath choke in his chest.

James let out a cry of horror and grief.

Vespasia touched the backs of her fingers to Iris's

85

neck, then looked up at Narraway. 'She's still breathing,' she said. 'But only just.' She turned to James. 'Go and get the first warm coat you can find. I suggest the garden room. And, Victor, you had better get the first manservant you encounter to come and help you carry her inside. Perhaps you would fetch the housekeeper as well. I dare say she's a practical person … they usually are.'

James was still standing, as if frozen. Narraway took him by the arm. 'Come on, there's no time to waste. Fetch anything you can find to wrap around her.' He grasped the young man's arm and pulled him until he came to life and swung round, barging out of the door, back into the conservatory, breaking into a run.

Narraway followed him, bent on finding the housekeeper, whatever she was doing, and getting help.

An hour and a half later, Iris was lying in the housekeeper's bedroom, wrapped in blankets and watched over by one of the maids, a middle-aged woman of great calm. The local doctor had been called and done all he could for her. She had not regained consciousness, and he was uncertain that she would, but she seemed to be resting quite easily and breathing regularly. The maid had instructions to remain with her at all times. If she needed to leave for any reason, she was to ring the bell and wait for a replacement. There was nothing else that could be done ... except wait.

Narraway told one of the footmen to stand watch outside the door.

'Yes, sir,' the man said gravely. 'Sir ...'

'Yes?'

'I heard gunshots last night, sir. At the time I thought it was poachers. They shoot in the woods around here sometimes. Not far, as the crow flies. I ... I know the boot boy heard them too. He told me, but ... I didn't like to say ...'

'I understand,' Narraway said quietly. 'I'm sure you're right about poachers. Sounds can seem so near in the night. Don't worry about it. Now, please look after Mrs Watson-Watt.'

'Yes, sir. Thank you, sir.'

Amelia came round the corner of the passage. She stopped in front of Narraway, ignoring the footman. 'Shouldn't we put her in her own bed?' she asked anxiously, for once all awareness of herself vanished. 'She will be far more ...' She searched for a word and could not find it. 'It's what she's accustomed to.'

'No,' Narraway said immediately. 'She should not be left alone at all.'

'But—'

'Lady Amelia, someone did this to her,' Narraway said sharply. 'It was to kill her, which he may yet succeed in. We must not—'

Amelia stiffened. 'Are you suggesting that one of my servants …?' she said indignantly.

He kept his patience with difficulty. 'No, I'm not. Possibly it was someone who broke in, but more likely it was one of us.'

'What on earth do you mean?' Now she was really angry, the colour burning up her face. But she was also frightened. 'What do you imagine gives you the right to come as a guest here and make appalling accusations like that? You are the only person here that I do not know! But I have given you the benefit of doubt, because I cannot imagine Vespasia would marry someone who was not fit to … be in decent society.' Her mouth twisted into a sneer. 'Although, as they say, there's no fool like an old fool!'

Narraway wished he could have hit her hard enough to knock her over. Instead, he looked at her icily. 'Her Majesty elevated me to the House of Lords because I rid her of a certain kind of vermin. A human rat catcher, shall we say. And clearly you are in need of one … however much you may dislike it.'

She swung her hand back, and before she could bring it forward and slap his face, he caught her wrist and held it hard, deliberately hurting her.

'An unpleasant thought,' he said very quietly. 'But it looks as if you have at least one rat in the house, Lady Amelia. You are lucky that Iris is still alive, and may well regain consciousness. It is not yet murder. I intend to see that it never is. Therefore, she will stay here, where there are people coming and going all the time. Maids, footmen, the cook, the house-keeper, boot boy, and anyone else who has sharp eyes and ears. Is that understood?'

'And who gave you the right to give orders in my house?' she demanded, but her voice shook with far more than anger. She lashed out in defence of everything she had. 'You are a guest here! And that because you have married above yourself!'

'Anyone who married Vespasia would be marrying above themselves,' he replied. 'I have suspicions that there is much we don't know behind the attack on Mrs Watson-Watt, and as I am a former Head of Special Branch, that gives me the right to take charge of this affair. Do you want to challenge that? Or would you rather we get to the bottom of this affair first, keep it discreet, and present it to the authorities when we have the answer? A *fait accompli*?'

Amelia snatched her hand back, rubbing her wrist and glaring at him with cold eyes. 'Take charge in *my* house? I shall see what my husband says.'

'Good idea,' Narraway agreed. He was certain Cavendish would not argue.

However, he was mistaken.

'We must call the police,' Cavendish replied without hesitation. They were standing alone in the chilly morning room. The fire had not been lit, and the room had a closed, unused feel to it, in spite of the luxury it offered. But it was the one place they could be certain of not being interrupted.

'And tell the police ... what?' Narraway kept his tone calm with difficulty. 'That Iris was in the orangery alone in the night, and one of the other guests attacked her and almost caused her death? May yet still do so, since we don't know if she will survive. And if she does, she will probably be able to tell us what did happen.'

'Don't be absurd!' Cavendish responded. 'Someone must have broken in. That's the obvious answer.'

'And what?' Narraway raised his eyebrows. 'Gone to the orangery to steal a ripe orange, if he could find one? At Christmas time? You think they'll believe that?'

Cavendish's face flushed. 'I don't know what the hell she was doing in the orangery. Presumably a tryst with someone ...'

'Who just happened to break into the orangery?' Narraway said incredulously.

'If it was a tryst, then by definition it was arranged,' Cavendish said. 'Don't be a fool!'

Narraway realised miserably that such a thing was not impossible, from Cavendish's point of view, at least. And probably anyone else's, who did not know the truth. In a way, it was exactly what had happened. She had gone there, by arrangement, to meet Narraway, just not for a romantic tryst. How was he going to get out of this? He had two possible courses. One was to allow Cavendish to bring the local police in, with all the accompanying scandal, and draw everyone's attention to the whole event, which would be disastrous to the Home Office, and everyone's reputations, especially if Iris did die. He did not want even to think of that. Alternatively, he could tell Cavendish an outline of the truth. It might not turn out well, but there was at least a chance it could.

91

Memories of Normandy washed over him like a deepening shadow. It was happening all over again. He had a taste in his mouth as bitter as gall.

'Cavendish ...' He swallowed. 'I'm obliged to tell you something that you probably would prefer not to know, but I have little choice.'

'Can't it—' Cavendish started to protest.

'No.' Narraway cut him off before he could finish.

Cavendish looked at Narraway more directly, studying his face and seeing the gravity in it. 'This had better be important, man! I can't think of any ...' He stopped. 'All right, what is it?'

Narraway struggled with how he was going to explain this, giving Cavendish as little information as possible It was a case of making the best of a bad job. And he must be quick. Cavendish's patience was about to snap at any moment. 'It's a Special Branch matter,' Narraway began.

'What?' Cavendish looked incredulous. 'Don't be absurd! This is a Christmas house party with a few people maybe you don't know, but Vespasia does. Don't make an ass of yourself, man ... more than you can help! God! You are a bloody outsider ...'

'It is a Special Branch matter,' Narraway repeated between his teeth. He hated this. He could feel the blood beating in his temples with the tension. This was Cavendish's house and, were Narraway in his place, he would have called the police both to guard himself and his family from the appearance of being involved, and perhaps to prevent any further attack. 'We must uncover the identity of Iris's attacker ourselves,' he hurried on.

'Someone tried to kill her,' Cavendish said bitterly. 'Special Branch is your only claim to success, and we can't check on that. It's all secret. You are little more than a jumped-up bloody policeman, and you can't do that effectively, or we wouldn't be in this mess. Are you saying you know who it is?' Cavendish was standing in the middle of the carpet, tense, as if he were about to let fly with some physical violence, even if only to relieve the tension boiling up inside him.

'I'm sorry,' Narraway said. 'It's an important—'

'Using my house was your idea?' Cavendish demanded. His face was twisted with disgust. 'I presume Lady Vespasia has no part in this … this squalid affair?'

'It's not squalid!' Narraway snapped. 'I don't know what makes you think it is! It is merely the passing over of information, but secretly, through a middle man, so the principal parties are not seen to meet.'

'Well, obviously you did it badly, since they did!' Cavendish said contemptuously. 'It's past time you retired. You've evidently more than lost your touch, and this is a damned disaster!'

Narraway felt the heat burning his face. Cavendish was right. He *had* lost his touch, except that Cavendish could not know it. But this was not the beginning of a decline, it was history tragically and terribly repeating itself. Narraway felt invaded by it, worn away from the inside. 'It's not a disaster yet. Iris is still alive.'

'For how long?' Cavendish said savagely. Then his expression changed to incredulity. 'My God! You want her kept here as bait! You want to capture your damned traitor and vindicate yourself, to hell with what happens to Iris! Or to the rest of us!'

It must look like that to him. Narraway could even see his point. It was like ice to his heart that Vespasia might even see it that way too, even for an instant.

Cavendish stared at him, outrage mottling his cheek.

'Iris will be safe now,' Narraway replied. 'We will see that there are people with her every minute.' Should he tell Cavendish the rest? He could not force his cooperation. He had to appeal for it. One of the guests here was to blame. Or very possibly two, though that was less likely. 'She doesn't have the information any more. I think that is fairly obvious. The danger is to someone else ...'

'Whoever took it from her?' Cavendish asked.

'Probably.'

The violent emotion was clear in Cavendish's face, but he controlled it with an effort Narraway could plainly see. 'Well, that at least explains why the Home Secretary nudged me into inviting Lady Vespasia, and so you came along as well. Believe me, it wasn't my idea. I thought he was asking me as some kind of favour to Lady Vespasia. That doesn't alter the fact that someone tried to kill Iris. Is whatever this is about worth her life?' His face darkened again. 'How dare you do this in my house! Damn you!' He took a deep breath and swallowed, then went on in a quieter tone. 'I suppose there's no point in cursing you, you're just the messenger boy. Look at you, at your age, carrying out errands like this ... and at Christmas. I imagine you have been invited to all sorts of people's houses, married to a real lady, not for your invented title to compensate you for losing your job. God in heaven! What have we come to?

95

Do I have to concede, or else be accused of not wanting to serve my country?'

'Yes,' Narraway agreed. He kept his temper in check with the greatest difficulty. 'That's about what it amounts to, because that's what it is. And for the record, the traitor is someone you invited, too, or Iris wouldn't be lying unconscious in your housekeeper's bedroom.'

'I find that hard to believe of my friends. Whoever it was, he was following you, no doubt!'

'Since I was the last to arrive, that seems unlikely.'

'Then I should blame whatever idiot is senior to you,' Cavendish swallowed. 'As I said before, you're only the lackey.'

'I prefer "frontline soldier",' Narraway said drily. 'Coming from a man who's no more than a bystander. But if "lackey" makes you feel better, by all means use it. Just don't bring in the police yet, and leave—'

'What?' Cavendish's eyebrows rose. 'You to clear this up? Really? Is there any chance you will be through by Easter?'

'I hope so. There are not many possibilities. It is either Dorian Brent, Rafe Allenby … or you. That shouldn't go beyond the New Year,' Narraway replied, with a certainty he did not feel.

Anger rose up Cavendish's face, and something else perhaps ... maybe alarm, as if he feared it might really last so long.

Narraway smiled. 'Perhaps with your assistance it will be less?'

'And how do you propose I explain what you suggest to my guests?' Cavendish asked. 'Shall I tell them Lord Narraway has it all under control? It is unnecessary to call in the regular police, whose profession it is to deal with attempted murder ... or if the poor girl dies ... actual murder?'

Narraway knew he was cornered. 'If she recovers, she may tell us who it was,' he began.

'Yes, I have thought of that.' Cavendish's voice was bitter. 'And no doubt whoever attacked her has thought of it also. Or is that your plan? Tempt him to try again? Hit her harder this time? Live bait, as it were? Is this what we've come to? And who are you going to set to guard her? Who are you certain is not guilty? Of course! Watson-Watt, the daydreaming artist. He wouldn't have the strength or the nerve.'

'Two people,' Narraway replied, ignoring the barbs. 'Servants, vouched for by your housekeeper, Mrs Pugh. One to watch the other.' His mind was racing. 'Didn't you think of that?'

97

'Get out!' Cavendish strode over to the door and opened it.

Narraway walked through without looking at him, as if Cavendish had been a servant doing the expected thing. Actually, his mind was already on how he would tell James. He had already dealt with Cavendish, as far as was possible.

He saw Amelia coming across the great hall with its inlaid marble floor, her soft leather shoes making little sound on it. She did not look pleased.

'This is appalling!' she said waspishly. 'What if the silly girl just slipped on a patch of mud?' She waved one hand dismissively. 'What was she doing in the orangery in the middle of the night anyway? Nothing any decent young woman would want us to know about. We should look the other way, and pretend we haven't seen … as you do when someone drops their false teeth in the soup!' She looked thoroughly annoyed.

Narraway wanted to laugh. He could feel hysteria rising up inside him, like a wave. It was so ridiculous, and yet sensible, and beyond his imagination to think of. 'I agree,' he said. 'Perhaps that was what happened. A guilty lover's secret, and she lost her balance? Do you think?' It was absurd enough to believe. For that matter, had she even seen whoever had hit her, or would she be as puzzled as the rest of them ... except one?

Amelia looked at him with some surprise. 'Well, what else? Either that ... or something equally idiotic. She's a young woman with too little to do, and too much taste to be the centre of everyone's attention. She should have some children. Or find something else useful to do.'

Narraway could think of no possible answer to that which wasn't rude, so he merely made a noise as if agreeing with her, and walked on quickly.

He eventually found James in the garden room, looking as if he were trapped inside the house and contemplating escape. Or that he realised that this was possibly the closest part of the house to the servants' quarters, and therefore to the housekeeper's room where Iris was lying, still unconscious. Those who were guarding her would not yet permit him any closer. He looked too frightened and too grieved to be angry about it. He was staring out of the window into the garden and did not appear to be aware that Narraway had come in and closed the door.

'James,' Narraway said gently.

James turned, blinking as if just waking up. 'What?

Has … has something happened?' His eyes implored to be told, and yet he was also terrified of the answer.

'She hasn't woken yet,' Narraway told him. 'I was looking for you because I had to tell you something in the utmost confidence. I cannot, unless you give me your word that you will not repeat it. Not only will you be prosecuted for treason if you do, but it may cost Iris her life. That you must believe, because it has already been attempted once.'

'What?' It was meant to be a demand, but his voice was too grating in his throat to have any authority.

Narraway took two overcoats off the pegs on the wall and handed one to James. 'Outside, and then we cannot be overheard.'

'Overheard? Who …?'

Narraway put his coat on and opened the door into the garden. He was immediately engulfed by icy air.

James obeyed, and several moments later they were a hundred feet along the path, with bare trees on one side and the cut-back herbaceous border on the other. A weak winter sun pierced the morning mist still shrouding some of the trees.

Narraway came immediately to the point. He had thought of exactly how much he would tell James, and what he must lie about, or just omit. 'Iris was carrying a package of immense importance to the Government,' he began. 'In order to pass it secretly to someone here and for them to take it on the next step of the journey. She did not tell you because she was sworn to secrecy for your protection, as well as her own.'

'Then how do you know?' James demanded. He was jerked out of his fear for her momentarily, and now he was angry, challenging. The most precious thing in his world had been threatened – indeed, might already be lost – and he was not going to believe anyone easily.

Narraway understood. He knew what it was to love so deeply, so certainly, that it was the light by which one saw everything else of value. Time did not reduce one's vulnerability. If anything, it made it greater. He answered with the truth. 'Because I am the one to whom she gave it. I have access to the people for whom it is destined, and she does not.'

'Then why didn't you take it in the first place?' James demanded. 'Why involve her at all?'

'Because she has easy and natural access to the people who had it in the first place. I do not,' Narraway replied.

'If it was meant to be secret, who attacked her,

and how did they know? Are they following you? And you led them to her?' There was sharp accusation in that. 'Even I know that you had something to do with Special Branch. That's more than unsubtle … it's just damn stupid!'

Narraway was stung, both because he was far above courier grade as much as the chief of all police was above the constable on the beat, and because there was sense in what James had said. Many people knew what he had been, probably most of the people who were guests in this house. It had even been mentioned. How should he answer? And had he been clumsy? Or was it a simple deduction anyone could have made. 'We assumed no one knew about the package,' he answered, trying to keep the edge of defensiveness out of his tone.

'Obviously someone did!' James snapped.

'Yes, I presume from the origins of the package. Whether they knew I was to receive it or not. They might not have known.

'Are you saying she was … careless?' James asked, his voice wavering now. He wanted to defend her, but he needed to know the truth. He was torn between needing Narraway's help, and wanting to blame someone other than Iris.

Narraway understood that. But he was far more used to having loyalties tested and his affections bruised than this young man. 'No,' he said quite honestly. 'If she was betrayed from the start, which is likely, then she did nothing wrong. She could have been perfect, and it would have made no difference.'

James walked in silence for several yards. A few last leaves drifted down from the branches above them and settled on the path.

'You must tell none of this, none at all, to anyone.' Narraway felt the urgent need to impress this on James. 'One person suspects, perhaps knows, but he also knows now that she did not have the package on her. It is not hard to deduce that she had passed it on already, to whomever it was intended, but they may well search your room.'

James stopped on the path and stared at him. 'I found my things had been slightly moved, just an inch or two. I noticed because my razor was just beyond my reach. I thought a maid had moved it. A shirt not hung up where I knew I had left it.'

'Precisely,' Narraway agreed. 'Nothing that would give you thought at the time. But be careful. Don't be alone, if you can help it. Have two people or more with you, and lock your room at night, if you are there.'

'But surely—'

Narraway put his hand on James's arm. 'It is one of the guests,' he said less gently. 'And let Iris stay where she is, in the servants' quarters, where the servants can be with her all the time.'

'Couldn't her attacker be one of them?'

'Whoever it is does this sort of thing very often,' Narraway pointed out. 'None of the servants is new here, except for a thirteen-year-old tweeny maid, about five-foot-nothing tall and ninety pounds dripping wet.'

James smiled bleakly, but there was gratitude in his eyes. 'Not her, then. Thank you for telling me. It does not really matter if she saw him, or if he thinks she might have, he will come back to kill her … if she lives. But …' he swallowed, '… it is better than thinking it was an assignation of some sort.'

Narraway looked back at him. 'She's perfectly charming, but I am sure it was not. The idea of betraying my wife with anyone at all is as sickening to me as it is to you. But I need you to help me, not get in the way.' That was only part of it. Narraway realised with surprise that it was also important to him to silence the agony of doubt in James's mind, the fear that the love that mattered so much to him was not real. Was it James he was protecting, or the belief in love itself?

He turned, and James turned with him. They walked slowly back along the way they had come towards the house, side by side, discussing what they could both do to help keep Iris safe.

Narraway had been afraid that this was the past, Normandy all over again, playing itself out and he was watching it as helplessly as before. It was not! But was it any better? There was still the unseen hand pulling all the strings, possibly bringing death to someone young, vibrant, so full of passion and hope, and he was watching just as uselessly.

Vespasia stood in the corner of the long gallery. It was a good place to be alone, while appearing to be engaged in looking at the portraits, mostly of Amelia's ancestors, going back to the Civil War two hundred and fifty years ago. They were colourful pictures. Artists loved painting the cavaliers – those aristocrats on the King's side – as handsome, romantic, with long curling hair, and hats with feathers, almost plumes, and of course lots of lace at the throat. The detail was ravishingly beautiful. And the cavaliers lost, which made them even more romantic. The roundheads were all plain and grim, with polished body armour, which reflected the light in interesting ways. They were pompous, humourless and self-righteous, and had wonderful names like Praisegod Barebones. Imagine addressing a child as Praisegod! They had to be humourless, or they would have tripped over themselves laughing! They won. No romance in that. Except for a satirist, perhaps? Vespasia felt there was a mine of ironic humour there, largely unexplored, to do with imposed religion and laughter; humour based upon the absurd.

But Amelia's ancestors had not run to satire. One eighteenth-century gentleman wore an expression as if he had bitten into a lemon, and carried the name Blessed Barbon. A descendent of Barebones, perhaps? Various other ancestors had gained their lands and titles for service to the restored king, Charles II, son of the beheaded Charles I, who was wise enough not to take revenge on those who had overthrown the Crown and executed his father. The Restoration was a time for the return of music, theatre, dancing again.

There was great wisdom in allowing people to laugh.

Vespasia realized she was deliberately escaping the present, and that had to stop. Narraway had not told her what he had been doing in the night, or what connection he had with Iris or the attack on her. However, it was apparent to Vespasia that it was extremely important to him. She assumed he would explain in time, and until then she must forget her own anxieties, the fear of being boring to him already, or at least insufficient to feed intelligence and the dreams that she knew lay deeper inside him than he had allowed anyone else to go. She must help him, blindly, if that were the only way open to her.

Who was Iris? More than a pretty young woman with a husband more interesting that he seemed at first? Who had attacked her, and why? Who was she to Narraway? Why had a couple so much younger than the rest of the guests been invited to this party at all?

No one had mentioned a family relationship. And there seemed no professional connection. Cavendish was a country gentleman with a marvellous estate, who sometimes dabbled in politics, possibly more than was visible in his easy-going manner.

Vespasia tried to recall all that she knew of him, but it was really no more than the tragedy of his first wife, Genevieve, hardly ever referred to. Cavendish had married again, although sometime after that. Lady Amelia Cavendish was a Cavendish born, as well as by marriage – a distant relation, apparently – and Cavendish Hall was hers. She had no living brothers, and so she had inherited it.

Rafe Allenby had an early military career, and a later one as an explorer, and finally as an ambassador in one or two unlikely places, mostly in the Middle East. Dorian Brent appeared to have inherited money, and done nothing remarkable himself.

What did Vespasia know about detecting? Nothing! She was an earl's daughter, wealthy enough never to have to concern herself with money. She knew and was known by everyone who was anybody. She had been loved, admired, envied, now and then hated. She had been an excellent horsewoman, a good shot, and above all passionately opinionated, and both physically and morally brave. All charming qualities, and utterly useless in the current situation.

And then her nephew had married the sister of Charlotte Ellison, who in turn had married Thomas Pitt, a policeman, of all things, and drawn them all into the world of crime and detection. Ultimately it had gone from Bow Street to Special Branch. Charlotte meddled in her husband's cases, and Vespasia had assisted her with intense pleasure, and as it turned out, considerable skill. Now it was time to think of Victor, and how she might put all of her past knowledge to use.

Of course, she could detect, if she put her mind and her heart into it. Proceed from the known to the unknown. But what did she know?

Iris had been attacked, very violently, in or near the orangery, sometime between midnight and about three in the morning. Was that certain? Yes. She was found in the orangery unconscious, with lacerations on her neck and shoulders. The blood from the cuts was already dry. She was fully dressed, stockings and shoes not even damp. She had not been outside, but she was not in her nightclothes. She was probably there to meet someone, planned beforehand.

She was badly hurt. The head injury was serious. In fact, she might die. Please heaven, not! But it was possible the attacker had meant to kill her, indeed might still mean to. It would be a good idea to go back to the orangery in full daylight and examine the place more clearly. For what? Signs of a struggle? Even a fight? Such as broken twigs or leaves on the ground, where they would not have fallen naturally. Scuffs in the earth around the orange trees. Signs of earth on the path, or marks on her shoes. Had anyone thought to tell the maid not to touch anything? Above

109

all, not to clean it? It was something she should do immediately, instead of standing here frozen in front of the portrait of Blessed Barbon, and the smell just under his nose, and maybe of temper, as if somebody, somewhere were laughing at him!

She went straight to the hall and across it, along the corridor and through the baize door into the servants' quarters. There was a footman outside the housekeeper's door, and he straightened as soon as he saw her.

'Sorry, m'lady, but you can't go in there,' he said unhappily.

'Quite right,' she approved. 'No exceptions. I would like to see the housekeeper, if you please.'

'Yes, m'lady.' He blushed. 'I can't take you, 'cause I've got to stay here, but you'll likely find Mrs Pugh in the butler's pantry. Everything's a bit …'

'Yes, of course it is. Thank you.' She went as she was directed and found the housekeeper, a slender woman with the customary large ring of keys tied to her apron at the waist.

'Yes, m'lady?' she said anxiously.

'If it hasn't already been done, will you instruct all the servants that they are not to enter the orangery?' Vespasia asked. 'I'm sure you appreciate we must examine the floor to see if there are any signs from which we can deduce what happened. In case there should be any ... difference of opinion. An innocent party may be blamed. It is all most unfortunate. How is Mrs Watson-Watt?'

'Still the same, m'lady. I don't know what else we can do for her,' Mrs Pugh said unhappily.

'Nothing but wait, I fear. When she comes round, she might take a sip of brandy, or hot beef tea.'

'We have both of them. Oh, I do hope she'll ...' She tailed off, not sure what else to say.

'So do I,' Vespasia agreed. 'We must hope for the best. Where are her shoes that she was wearing at the time? If you have not cleaned them ...'

'No time yet, m'lady.'

'Excellent. May I see them, please?'

'Certainly. If you'll just wait ...'

'I'd rather come with you. I want to see them exactly as they are, before any dirt or smudges are knocked off them, or wiped away.'

The housekeeper gave her a momentary look of confusion but she obeyed. They were in the house-keeper's room where Iris was still lying motionless, face white, eyes closed.

Vespasia hesitated a moment, looking at Iris,

saying a silent prayer, and then moved to the shoes. 'Very good place to keep them,' she approved. 'Are the rest of the clothes here?'

'Over there, m'lady.' Mrs Pugh pointed to where they were carefully laid over the back of the chair.

Vespasia went across to the shoes first and looked at them closely. First the left foot. She turned it over. The sole was quite dry, but there was a shred of mulch on the heel. She looked at the other and found a deep scar on the heel, as if it had been drawn hard and heavily sideways across some sharp edge. If Iris's shoe had been on her foot at the time the scar was made, she must have fallen hard against the concrete edge of the surround to one of the orange trees.

Did that indicate anything they did not already assume?

Vespasia began examining the clothes, picking them up one by one, turning them to the light to see if there were tears, holes, smears of soil, or blood. There was very little to see: a bit of loose mulch on the hem of her gown, hard to distinguish because of its dark shade. There was no blood anywhere, even on the shoulder near her head where she had bled, though not heavily. Was there blood on someone else's clothes? Would they hide it? Or try to wash it out? Or get rid of it? That was a line to follow. How much blood was it?

What could the attacker do? Deliberately cut a finger to account for it? That was something to look for?

Had he intended to kill her but not hit her hard enough? Would he wait, go back to complete the act? Even if only to suffocate her while she was unconscious and could not fight, scream, or defend herself in any way?

Maybe he had not meant to kill her. So was rendering Iris unconscious an accident or clumsiness? What effect had that on him? Or his plans? Surely Victor would question all the servants, especially the ones who would have noticed marks on clothes. What would the guests have to say about each other? That might be most telling, if the questions were clever enough.

Would Victor tell her any progress he made? Should she ask, or would that only invite rebuff?

'Come on!' she told herself grimly. Hurt feelings were small and absurdly self-important now. Whether he wanted her help or not, Victor might need it very much. There would be time for apologies afterwards.

113

She thanked the housekeeper and took her leave, going back upstairs. She was not yet ready to face Narraway. She wanted all the information she could acquire before she tried to put it together.

She was upstairs in her room, looking for a clean white lace fichu to add a little warmth, when her fingers touched a package she did not recognise. She hesitated for a moment, then pushed away the handkerchiefs that were close to it, and another lace collar and a silk fichu. They left in her hand a tightly wrapped packet the size of a large business envelope, but it was not paper, rather it was carefully wrapped oiled silk, with a seal on it. She had never seen it before.

Had Victor put it there? There was no reasonable alternative. She wrapped it again in the silk fichu, then disguised its shape with lace collars and a piece of feminine underwear she hoped no one else was likely to undo.

She stood up slowly and went to the window, because she needed to see high above her the wind-driven clouds across the sky and feel the sense of space. This house in all its extravagance and unhappiness was closing in around her. Only Victor could have put the package where it was. It was possibly the best place to hide it, and whatever it contained. But it was now obvious that the reasons for which he had come to Cavendish Hall this Christmas were very important. There could be many of them, good or bad, but it was the possibility of the bad ones that hurt, like a thorn not jagged on the surface of the skin where it could be pulled out, but inside, where it would hurt until it grew septic and poisoned the blood.

There had been years of life before they met each other, time that had to contain things they might never know. She had thought it did not matter. She had thought they were trivial, the facts that had forged who they were now, and the particulars were unimportant. Perhaps she had been wrong.

But Iris's injuries, perhaps her death, would not permit such luxury of ignorance. She turned away from the window and went out of the room and downstairs. She found Narraway in the withdrawing room talking to Dorian Brent.

She smiled charmingly at Dorian, then turned to Narraway. 'I think it might rain later on. Would you accompany me for a walk in the garden before that?' It was phrased as a question but it was not really one. She would not accept a refusal.

'Of course,' Narraway answered, and excused himself to Dorian.

They walked in silence to the garden room, put on boots and coats, then went outside into the sharp chill air.

'It's not going to rain,' he observed.

'Not yet.' It was a polite fiction. 'I was looking for a white lace fichu ...'

He stared straight ahead and kept walking at a slow, even pace.

'I found the package which I believe you put there,' she continued. 'I cannot imagine anyone else hiding such a thing in my undergarments.'

There was a faint flush in his cheeks, more than that stung by the wind. 'It was the safest place to put it. I apologise if I ... intruded.'

'Don't be absurd!' she snapped. 'I have no secrets in there! Is it what you took from Iris?'

'Took from? No, it is what she gave me,' he corrected.

'What you came here to collect, if you prefer.'

'Yes.' He continued to look straight ahead. 'She gave it to me, and I thought she had left. Either I was mistaken, or she left and came back ...' His voice trailed off.

116

'And someone attacked her.'

He swung round to face her. 'For God's sake, you don't think that I did, do you?'

It was a genuine question. She saw it plainly in his eyes. She controlled herself with an effort. This was not the time to follow through with all the unanswered questions that boiled upwards inside her, raw, painful, but never of suspecting him of such a thing. Perhaps it was herself she doubted? But this was not about her. Solve this first! Then, if the pain remained, pull it out and take it apart. 'No, I don't,' she said with as much self-control as she could manage. 'I don't imagine you doing that at all, least of all here, and now, a few days before Christmas.' Her voice wavered and she hated her own vulnerability. 'You are doing something that is very important to you, and you have not told me what it is, and I am not trying to guess.' Did that sound petty, as if she were concerned about hurt feelings of being excluded more than the importance of what it meant to him? Or to the country? It was a time when she must be better than that. She swallowed and took a breath. 'And it is clearly dangerous. Iris was nearly killed over it. She yet may be. The package is critical. You may be next. Or I may be.'

117

'No!' His voice was almost strident. He took her by the arms, at first roughly, then as she winced, loosening his hold. 'You are not involved.'

She forced her voice to be gentle, although her feelings were far from it. 'I appreciate being protected, if that is your intent, but it is a little late for—'

'Of course that was my intent! What else could it be?'

She knew from his eyes, impenetrably dark, shielded, that that was not the whole truth. 'But it is too late for that now,' she finished. 'I am aware that you do not know who your enemy is.'

'No. But the choice is limited.' He started to move again, slowly, perhaps to seem to be doing no more than taking a walk, in case they were being observed.

It gave her a cold feeling quite different from that of the chill morning air with a dampness in it of coming rain. 'We had better be more precise,' she said. 'This needs to be solved before anyone else is hurt. Don't shut me out, Victor. You can't protect me, except by solving this.'

For a moment, they kept walking. They had reached the end of the herbaceous border and the path went through an arch that would be covered with roses in the spring, but just now only the bare stems wound through the trellis. In front of her was a flight of shallow steps with a balustrade on either side, beautiful carved urns on the pedestals at both ends.

They crossed the path and started upwards, still side by side.

'I really have no idea who it is,' he said when they reached the top.

'Then we had better think hard,' she replied. 'And don't waste time putting me off. I am staying, with you or alone. I think we can omit James Watson-Watt. That leaves everyone else. Is there anybody you can exclude because of the nature of … whatever it is?'

'No.'

She racked her mind, trying to recall everything she knew of the different women who were here. What passions or griefs lay beneath the polite, well-trained smiles?

She had seen a pain in Amelia she had never recognised before. Had it been there all the time, masked by retaliation against – anyone? Perhaps, for a proud woman, being pitied was worse than being disliked by an equal? But pitied for what? For being bullied, perhaps, in her own house? For being frightened, even for being unloved? Who knew what went on in someone else's marriage?

119

And Rosalind Allenby? Did she feel excluded from all Rafe's former adventures, many of which Vespasia had shared, at least in part? But that had nothing whatever to do with Iris, except that Allenby seemed so attracted to her.

And that hardly seemed reason enough to attack her so violently! Had Rosalind, or anybody, imagined that Iris was going to the orangery to meet someone romantically?

And Georgiana Brent? Was the feeling of exclusion – and Vespasia had seen it in her face for more than an instant – such as anyone might feel? Such as Vespasia herself felt, in this particular house party?

'Victor?' she prompted. 'Could the assailant be a woman, out of jealousy, perhaps? Rather than anything at all to do with the package?'

He hesitated and turned to face her, immediately masking his features. 'No,' he said sharply.

'Don't be intentionally stupid!' she answered impatiently. 'Women have killed before, and jealousy is one of the oldest reasons in the world. If someone followed, whoever it was … no, that would make no sense …'

'None at all,' he said with a shadow of a smile. 'Or are you suggesting that Iris had a meeting with me, to give me the package, at midnight in the orangery, and someone else had an assignation with Iris, or with someone else, at midnight in the orangery, and by extraordinary mischance, the person, consumed with jealousy, struck Iris by mistake, and both the other two escaped unseen and unheard? That means four of us, all in the orangery at midnight, and we did not see each other? It's a big orangery, but that's absurd. Was anybody in bed?'

She wanted to laugh and cry at the same moment. She kept herself controlled with great difficulty. 'Well, Iris was definitely there. And you admit you were. If you did not strike her, then someone else was there, too. Or are you suggesting she went down again, at a later time? Why? A genuine assignation this time?' She heard the disbelief in her own voice.

She saw his jaw tighten, an expression she knew well.

They were walking slowly, actually in step. Without realising it, he had matched his pace to hers. The air was damp, smelling of fresh earth.

She knew it was up to her to speak. 'Is there anyone you know well enough to rule out? If we could narrow it down, it might help.'

'I suppose we should concentrate on the men,' he

121

replied after a moment. 'It was clearly someone strong enough to overcome Iris and attack her, but why?'

'The package?' she asked. Then her mind slipped back to her examination of Iris's dress on the back of the chair. 'No, it might have been to force her to say who she gave it to.'

He looked at her curiously. 'Why do you say that?'

'Iris was very slim, and there was definitely no place in her dress where she could have concealed a package of that size. Anyone with observation at all would know that. Or have you considered that it might have nothing to do with the package? Who else would know about it, anyway?'

'Only someone involved in the same espionage …' He said it slowly, as if it had greater meaning than he had first thought.

'What?' she asked.

He said nothing.

'Victor?'

'I was just thinking of something that happened long ago. In some ways, it was a bit like this.'

So, this was digging deeper memories again, something he had not told her about. There were many things in her life that she had not told him, and probably never would. Some of them were painful, many were happy, but they belonged in the past, and to other people, people he would never know.

She decided to put her own emotions aside and return to the subject. 'Anything in those memories that could be helpful to this?' she asked, keeping the emotion out of her voice as much as she could.

'The passing of another package.' His voice caught. 'Another young woman ... but she was killed.'

'I'm sorry.' She needed to say something in the silence. How could she ask how it was related to this? 'You were there?'

'Yes.' He stared straight ahead of him. The lines of his face were tight and hard. Full of grief.

She was shut out of this old memory, but the wave of emotion that swept over her was not jealousy, or any kind of feeling of exclusion, only the passionate need to protect him from it ever happening again. The past, she knew, was unreachable. 'Iris isn't dead, Victor, and we can solve this. But we need to be clear-headed. It happened at a country house party?'

'Yes, in Normandy, in the middle of summer. There is no place more deeply, richly beautiful, more certain of its ... of its own completeness. Do you know what

I mean?' He glanced at her, then away again, but that instant he had shown a need for her to understand.

'Yes,' she said. 'I've been to Normandy in the summer, and further south … vineyards in the sun, making a sweet wine of their tears. The summer fades, but the taste remains.'

He said nothing.

She brought him back to the present. 'How did it end? Who was responsible?'

'I never found out. I … failed.'

So that was it. It was more than grief; it was unfinished in his mind. Above everything, she must not be clumsy. She must acknowledge it so he never afterwards doubted her understanding. Nor would she ask him what his part in it had been.

'Could this be connected – other than by coincidence? Are any of the same people involved?'

'Not that I know of. Normandy was twenty years ago.'

Was it hope in his voice? Or just overwhelming weight of the pain of remembrance?

'Then if not, perhaps it has nothing to do with the package. Consider what else it might be. Are you satisfied that the attacker was not James?'

'Yes, why? Do you think it could have been?' He

turned towards her, and then suddenly away again. 'Have I missed something?'

'I don't think so. It is just that anyone we can disregard leaves fewer to consider. Have you any idea who the enemy is? Nationality he sympathises with? Unusual skills? Other events like this that might tell us something more about him? How would he know that Iris was going to give something to you?' She knew that perhaps she was on dangerous ground, but there was no retreating now. 'It has to be someone who knows you, doesn't it? Did they also have to know the courier was Iris?'

He was silent for several steps. They were walking without taking the slightest notice of where they were going. 'I don't think whoever it was followed me,' he answered thoughtfully. 'But I suppose he could have. Which means he was waiting, and followed me downstairs and along the gallery to the orangery. There's no furniture in the gallery. Nothing to hide behind, if I had turned. How on earth could he explain himself?'

'Then he waited, and followed Iris,' she replied. 'Even so, he took a chance.' She concentrated on the gallery in her mind's eye. 'There are gas lamps there. A few. Were they lit? I mean, all of them?'

'No … not all of them.' He faced her. 'You mean he deliberately turned some of them off, at the base of each burner. He must have done that every night.'

She gave a shiver at the forethought of it. What was behind all this? Was it devotion to another country, another cause? Or hatred of England? How could anyone mask that so well? Without thinking of it, she wrapped her coat more tightly around her.

He reached out and for a moment held her. Then, as if recalling himself back to the moment, let his hand fall.

She swallowed back the words that rose and replaced them carefully with ones that were relevant. 'If you're convinced it must be one of the men then it is Brent, Allenby or Cavendish. Knowing it would be helpful, but we have to prove it also. And tomorrow is Christmas Eve…'

He said nothing.

Somewhere above them a bird flew out of a tree and rode the billowing wind up into the sky.

'Would his wife know?' She pursued her own thoughts. 'Or guess?'

He smiled, as if something were both funny and sad. 'I doubt it. Most of us really do not know each other very well.'

'A lot of women know their husbands a great deal better than their husbands would like to believe,' Vespasia said drily. 'I think she would know there was a lot about her husband that was not what people supposed. But she would think it was a mistress, or even a lover of the same sex …'

He stared at her, but she ignored him.

'… or an opium habit, or gambling. Drinking she would know about. It is usually more obvious. And another thing, is he doing this out of idealism, love or hatred? Or is he being pressured into it because of some unfortunate secret? That makes a difference.'

'Does it?' Narraway said bleakly.

'Yes. An idealist is different from a man terrified.' She stopped. It was an appalling thought, but the more she considered it, the sharper and more real it became. She remembered past experiences of people who behaved in a way that only became understandable when one knew the entire story: the loves, the fears, even the old losses. 'Who's the real enemy, Victor?'

'I don't know,' he admitted very quietly. 'That's the worst of it. I'm not sure if his purpose is to give misinformation to us or whether it's giving information to the enemy …which is probably Germany. It's the biggest rising naval power likely to threaten us. Or maybe this is personal, to take some kind of revenge on me or the Home Secretary.'

She did not reply. There was nothing to say. She wanted to take his hand and let him know she understood, without words that were too direct, too clumsy at this moment, but she was not sure enough that he would welcome them.

She started to walk again, slowly, matching her steps to his.

The rest of the day went according to Amelia's plan for her guests, except that, of course, neither Iris nor James was present. It was all rather forced, but no one wished to raise the question that hung in the air. Women wrote letters, men played billiards, or read in the library. In ordinary circumstances, it would have been restful and perhaps a little boring. They would catch up on old friendships, new gossip.

Vespasia went for another walk in the garden, ignoring the fine rain, because she wished to be alone to think. Anything she might learn from Rosalind, Amelia, or Georgiana was unlikely to be relevant, and there was no time to be oblique. And frankly, she was too worried to disguise her enquiries in the usual meaningless chatter. She was older than any of the women, and today she felt it. It was not a tiredness or an aching in the bones, but an awareness of the reality of treason, and attempted murder, and a certain darkness that threatened them all. Particularly, it threatened Victor, and in ways that he was not prepared to share with her. There was no use arguing with him. It would only increase the division between them, and apart from the pain of that, which was deep and raw, it would stop them working together.

Deducing was fine, when they had lots of information and could gather more, and time to spare. They had not. After Christmas, they would part and all go to their own homes. But far more pressing than that, Iris was still in danger, if there were any chance at all that she had seen who had struck her. And that was the other thing! Who else might be in danger? They needed to know what this was about.

And maybe she needed to know about the past episode that had ended tragically, and which had left such a deep and still aching scar on Victor.

Of one thing she was certain: the present danger

of violence must be dealt with first. She walked in the opposite direction from this morning, around the lawn with its damp earth and grass long enough to wet her boots and the hem of her skirt. She was going towards the large lily pond, bare of flowers now, but it must be surpassingly lovely in the summer. She stood on the gravel and watched the wind shivering across the smooth surface of the water, then in a lull, ironing it out to be grey-brown until the next fan of breeze troubled it. How deep did it go? An inch? Two inches? And that's all she and Victor were doing with the problem: tickling the surface.

They must dig deeper, in all the places a clue might be. Someone in the house had known Iris would keep her appointment. Had she simply told them where and when? She spoke to everyone quite openly. There was no need for coded messages. She just must not be seen handing anyone a package. It was large enough to be conspicuous. Someone would be bound to comment. There was no way to explain it and keep it secret that was reasonable.

James did not know anything about it, and he was inclined to be jealous, even if Narraway was twice his age. Iris was not the first young woman Vespasia had seen show a personal interest in Narraway. He was lean, elegant, so sure of himself on the outside, that he exuded power. He was clever, and wise enough to hide it most of the time. And he could be both sensitive and funny. He loved great art, whether it was music, literature or painting, and he did not conceal his acute pleasure in it.

Would she have fallen in love with him when she was less than thirty? Quite possibly. And would he have found her beautiful, interesting, used her lightly and then moved on? Yes, that was possible too. And would she have forgotten him? Perhaps not.

It was better now, when they were both wiser and gentler, daring to drink deep of their emotions, care and admit it. And she would still be hurt.

But Iris was lying unconscious in the housekeeper's room, guarded as well as could be. And whoever had struck her would doubtless try again to find the package. He had only to look thoroughly enough. Would he do it himself? Or ask his wife to? Would she agree? Was she part of it? Or could he think of a suitable lie as to why she should do such a thing? Would Vespasia do that, if Victor asked her? She did not know the answer to that. It was another thought to consider. A man alone? Or a man and his wife willingly? A man and a wife coerced?

And why did he do this, anyway? Loyalty to another power? Blackmail? Some deep, personal vengeance or hatred? They were all different, and might lead to different paths.

She saw dimples of rain on the surface of the pond. The air was colder. It was time to get back to the house. She turned and walked with the wind behind her, pushing her a little. She had come without a hat and it was pulling at her hair. She would have a pot of tea sent up to her bedroom while she tidied herself.

She was in the bedroom before the mirror when Narraway came in. She had dried her hair and was pinning it back up again.

'I got caught in the rain,' she explained.

'You were out!'

She looked at his eyes in the mirror and did not bother to reply.

He sat on the bed, watching her. It was something that pleased him, even now. 'Why did you go out?'

She heard the tone of his voice. It was a demand for an explanation based on anxiety, not a perceived right to know. 'To think clearly,' she replied. 'Without having to make idiotic conversation. Some people find it comforting, but …'

'Women talk such rubbish.' He dismissed it. 'How can anyone at a time like this, with Iris … Even if they know nothing else, they know someone is violent! And …'

She turned round, facing him across the deep, rich bedroom carpet. 'You are listening to the words, Victor. They don't matter. If a man speaks, they have something to say. But with a woman, it is not the words, it is the message that matters: *I am concerned for you, I like you. I understand.* Or, *you can trust me. I am listening.* Whether it comes out as nonsense is not the point.' She looked at him steadily. 'Do you really not know that? Or are you testing to see if I know it too?'

He looked startled for an instant, then he decided to be honest. 'No, I wasn't aware of that.'

Vespasia swallowed what she had been going to say, and even kept her eyebrows from rising in incredulity. 'Just like men boasting to each other. I imagine that translates roughly like gorillas beating their chests.'

He really did not want to, and it was plain in his face, but he could not help laughing. 'I had no idea you saw us in such farmyard terms.'

'Gorillas in the farmyard?' This time her eyebrows

did go up. 'Really, Victor. This is nothing so alarming. It is the jungle. And you know that even better than I.'

The laughter vanished and he was very serious again. 'And the chaos of the jungle is a part of life, but we need to understand it.'

'And we need to understand the people in it,' she replied. 'First, find a better place for the package. This man will search our room soon enough. The question is, will he do it himself, or will he ask his wife to do it? Does she know who or what he is? And would she help him, willingly or unwillingly? Or will he bribe a servant? Either is dangerous, unless his wife shares his belief.'

'Or understands the threat to him,' he added. His voice sank even lower, as if saying it more softly robbed it of some of its power. 'There are several motives for treason, apart from idealism. There is money, fear of exposure for something, and sheer hatred of those you feel have slighted you, passed you over or – more honourably, I suppose – those you believe have betrayed their allegiances by denying their own code in something. I've seen that.' A cloud crossed his face. 'Had to execute a man whom I admired more than I did those whom he betrayed.

It's an old story.' But it was clearly one that still mattered to him.

She did not question him further. 'Don't tell me where you put it, just take it from here. They'll look, they're bound to, and if we caught them it would be very helpful.'

He tensed. 'Vespasia! You are not to hide it! You are not to pretend to hide it! Do you hear me?'

'Of course I hear you!' she replied. She swallowed her indignation. She knew the comment came from fear. It was in his eyes, in his rigid hand on the lush coverlet of the bed where he was leaning. 'Nor, I think, will I spend much time in the room alone,' she added. 'It is nearly time we changed for dinner. They have to search in here. It is the perfect bait. But wherever you hide it, be careful! Whoever this man is, he is perfectly capable of following you and killing you, and making it look like an accident.'

'You don't need to spell it out! I have been doing this for years.' His voice was not hard-edged; it was more sadness than a boast. 'Please, for my sake if not your own, be more careful yourself!' He seemed about to add something. There was a flicker of humour in his eyes, as if he had been going to lighten the mood for a moment, then changed his mind. 'I

135

don't know whether not telling you where I put it lessens your danger or increases it.'

'Lessens it,' she said immediately.

He looked grim. 'If you know, then at the worst threat, you could tell them.'

She stood up. 'Victor, don't be an ass. You, of all people, are a realist. Don't protect me as if I were a child and couldn't work it out for myself. If it comes to that, and they kill me if I don't tell them, then if I do they will kill me afterwards.'

'I'm sorry …' He looked wretched.

'Don't be!' she said gently, realising she was now afraid, too. She walked past him, round the end of the bed into the middle of the rose-coloured carpet. 'I'm your wife, not your child! If you talk down to me, I shall slap you. If you've forgotten, I fought at the barricades in Rome during the revolution of '48. You wouldn't know about that.' She was deliberately reminding him of the one fact she hated, that she was considerably older than he. 'And I slap very hard indeed!' she added. She let her breath out slowly. 'I think I shall wear the grey and silver gown, with diamonds, this evening. It is a colour Amelia likes, and it suits me far better than it does her. It will infuriate her.'

'And you want to do that?' he said slowly, not sure whether to laugh or not.

'Of course I do.' She looked at him over her shoulder. 'People make mistakes when they're angry. If you lose your temper, you also lose your judgement.'

He stood up as well. 'We can't rely on other people's mistakes.'

'No, but we can certainly use them!'

Dinner was magnificent, as if everyone were deliberately denying that anything at all could be wrong. The room was decorated in wine red, the shade of the velvet winter curtains. There were golden balls attached to all the silk-tasselled swag ropes. Red candles burned on the mantel, and on the table, set, of course, with silver candelabra. Light gleamed on crystal goblets, and on the magnificent array of silver knives, forks, spoons, soup spoons, dessert forks and four sets of cruets.

The flowers in three vases were red and gold chrysanthemums, smelling exquisitely of damp earth. It would almost be a shame to overwhelm them with the aroma of food.

The company took their places in silence, the ladies each assisted by a footman.

Iris was still unconscious. James was sitting at her bedside, watching, willing her to come back to him. The housekeeper would take him supper on a tray.

Amelia was dressed in warm glowing shades, which flattered her remarkably. She wore the Cavendish rubies, very expensive and very beautiful. She smiled at Vespasia. 'Charming,' she murmured. 'Grey is so … so … discreet.'

Vespasia turned slightly so her diamonds flashed in the blistering light of the chandelier. 'So generous of you,' she murmured. 'I'm sure Christmas is going to be wonderful.'

Cavendish sat at the opposite end of the table from Amelia. He looked steady, totally calm on the outside. 'I'm glad that distressing events did not drive you away, Lady Vespasia. I was so afraid you would feel compelled to leave early. It could not possibly be the same pleasure without you.'

That caught Vespasia by surprise. 'For such an unfortunate event, one does not abandon one's friends,' she replied with a gentle smile. 'I wouldn't dream of leaving.'

The colour flushed up Amelia's face. Contrastingly, Cavendish went white. What did he feel, or know, that Amelia did not?

Vespasia smiled even more graciously, but the difference intrigued her. She had not thought Amelia and Cavendish antipathetic to each other. There had always been some tension there, but she had supposed it was due to the fact that both the title and the money were hers. Now she recognised that it was more than that. But what? The petty things that became annoying over time, or something major, blocking out the light?

She was risking being rude to Rosalind Allenby by remaining half turned away from her, even though it was in order to face Amelia. It was easy to do because Rosalind was a quiet woman, almost serene, as if she knew some inner security that was a secret to others. Like the Mona Lisa, Vespasia thought ruefully. Was Rosalind actually like Vespasia herself, with an iron discipline to appear warm and charming on the outside, and invulnerable, perfect as an evening sky, and yet underneath as capable of pain, doubt and loneliness as anyone else? Could you have raging winds underneath a stainless sky? Of course! Why not? Perhaps Rosalind Allenby hid far more than she revealed.

'Shall we have snow, do you think?' she said to Rosalind. 'It's so beautiful at first, but like fresh fish, it is less charming by the third day.'

139

Rosalind smiled back, a sudden warmth in her face. 'I'm so glad you didn't say "like house guests"! They, too, are supposed to wear rather thin by that time, so the saying goes.' Her eyes were sparkling with inner life, clashing thoughts she probably never gave voice to.

'Good or not, I think it will be a Christmas we shall not forget,' Vespasia replied. 'However much we might try …' she added.

'Please don't say that!' Rosalind begged.

'I'm sorry.' Vespasia was taken aback.

'You'll make me laugh,' Rosalind explained.

'Oh.' Vespasia let out her breath in a sigh.

They continued the conversation with considerable pleasure. Vespasia knew quite a lot about Allenby himself, and shared her knowledge through a delicate and warm series of anecdotes, some merely a sentence long. She appreciated that Rosalind loved him, even though she was perfectly aware of his shortcomings. It was a health issue that she did not travel with him, but he wrote her long descriptive letters, sharing not only where he was, but the feelings it awoke in him.

Vespasia had seen the courage in him, the physical endurance, and the intellectual curiosity. She had not seen what Rosalind had: his pleasure in sharing with her the beauty unnoticed by others, the delight in artistic workmanship in the simplest objects, the patience with a stubborn or frightened animal. He was not ashamed of that side of his nature, but perhaps a little embarrassed by it.

And Rosalind protected him by her silence. Theirs was a subtle relationship, but Vespasia understood it instinctively. Perhaps there was something of Victor in Allenby? Moments of tenderness that he had guarded, seeing them as vulnerability, not strength. How many people were so ill-understood? On the other hand, how many were regarded as more, when the only wisdom they possessed was to keep tight the covers over their emptiness?

Conversation was sparse. Recent events lay heavily over the party. No one was prepared to pretend that James had attacked Iris, which meant the absurd fiction that some unseen person had broken into the house in the middle of the night and then gone without trace to the orangery where there was nothing to steal, not even any ripe oranges. And who would prefer that to all the wealth of art and trinkets lying around the rest of the house? Any alternative supposed that Iris had also gone to the orangery alone, in the middle of the night … and what innocent purpose would answer that? An assignation with a stranger was possible, but no one believed it. The only credible alternative was that someone at this table was guilty.

It was only when Cavendish himself finished his dessert and began to speak that Vespasia realised with dawning horror that Narraway was the one most reasonably to be suspected.

'You must find life very quiet, Narraway, now that you've retired?' Cavendish remarked. 'I don't see you as a man who moves from one house party to the next. I always perceived you as someone who did not go anywhere without a purpose …' His voice trailed off, as if the words were a question and required an answer.

Georgiana Brent looked at Narraway curiously. She clearly had no idea that he had until recently been Head of Special Branch, or what that would mean. For obvious reasons, it was not an appointment made public. Cavendish was being indiscreet.

Everyone was waiting for an answer.

Vespasia glanced at Cavendish. She saw no humour or innocence in his eyes. In fact, there was something bright and hard, which she read with a chill as malice.

Why? Personal? Professional? Social, because Narraway also had married an earl's daughter, but had finally achieved a title all his own? It was ridiculous, but she knew men who had hated for less.

Narraway was being too slow to answer, and yet if she answered for him the implication was there that she believed he would not match wits with Cavendish himself.

Everyone had stopped eating. There was no clink of silver on porcelain. Only the movement of a hand caused the chandelier to glint on a diamond on a wrist, or finger.

'What man would not wish to be in society every so often, if they could take Lady Vespasia on their arm each time?' Narraway said with a smile, to rob it of the vulgarity of boasting. Nevertheless, the pride was there.

Was it an act? Surely. Narraway was not a vain man, nor a brash one, so it must be a barb returned, to let Cavendish, and anyone else, know that the battle was real, sharp and he was able for it. Amelia was not a woman one took anywhere to show off, either for her beauty or her wit. She was adequate, reliable – words of value, but damning to the vanity. Vespasia said nothing, but winced inwardly. She felt

143

a fleeting moment of pity, but shrugged it off. There was no place for a lapse of attention.

The silence seemed to overcome everything.

'Here was I, thinking we were complimented by your presence,' Cavendish replied at last, looking at Narraway. 'When all you wanted was a chance to be seen. Aren't you a little … mature … to be doing that? Or perhaps *mature* is not the right word. But the right word would be *old*, and that would be unkind at best.'

'I'm sure you would never be unkind!' Vespasia said before she could stop herself. She had not meant to defend him. 'It is so revealing of unhappiness, a sense of failure.'

Rosalind drew her breath in sharply.

Georgiana choked, but it sounded extraordinarily like laughter.

To Vespasia's surprise, it was Amelia who rescued the situation, or at least she who filled the silence.

'I invited Vespasia, naturally including her husband.' She looked at Cavendish witheringly. 'I compose the guest list for such occasions, and Christmas is rather special, don't you agree? A time for healing old wrongs, settling old debts?' She looked round the table at each of them in turn, not saying whether she meant paying, or collecting! 'And Cavendish Hall is such a perfect place for doing it. There is plenty of room to be both independent and yet together.' Her face wore a look of deep pride, as if she had slipped back a hundred years and her side of the family still ruled half the county.

Vespasia remembered telling Narraway before they came that Amelia had both the title from her father, and the money from her mother, as she was now obliquely reminding Max.

'The house is perfect,' Vespasia dropped into the momentary silence. 'And I have never seen lovelier gardens. Even at this time of the year, it is a pleasure to walk in them.'

'I would not walk in them alone.' Cavendish suddenly rejoined the conversation. 'There appears to be someone among us with a strong predisposition to violence, especially against women.'

Vespasia turned to look at him. His face wore an expression of concern, warning, and yet she saw a threat also. His clenched hand rested on the white embroidery of the tablecloth. Was her imagination running away with her? That was no use at all. One of these people had tried to kill Iris, and could yet succeed. Why?

She smiled at Cavendish. 'So, you don't think that Iris was attacked for a personal reason, or because she's young and beautiful and perhaps indiscreet?'

He was startled.

'Well, unfortunately I am no longer any of these things.' She went on, as if it concerned her. 'And I have no idea who's guilty, so I would not be attacked to keep me silent.'

'Have you not?' he asked. 'I had heard you meddled considerably in the cases of Sir Thomas Pitt, when he was a policeman, before he was … elevated … to the peerage. A gamekeeper's son. The wretched father was transported to Australia, I believe. They are elevating all sorts of people these days.'

Vespasia was seething. The insult to Pitt, whom she admired profoundly and loved almost as a son, was a step too far. She looked Cavendish up and down with a cold, raking eye, and before Narraway could interrupt she said quietly, 'Not quite all sorts.' She thought of adding, *There are still a few beyond the pale*, but decided against it.

Narraway was across the table from her and could only meet her eye, not touch her, but the fury within him was palpable.

The butler, who perhaps had heard the remark, or at least felt the prickling silence around the table, signalled the footmen and parlour maid to clear the table and serve the liqueurs.

Cavendish leaned towards Vespasia. 'Not to keep you silent, perhaps, but simply for the pleasure of it,' he whispered.

'Did that apply to Iris, too?' she asked after a second's delay. 'Your pleasure? Or did she refuse you?'

'As you have observed, Lady Vespasia, you and Iris Watson-Watt have nothing in common,' he retorted. 'There must be, among other things, half a century's age between you.'

'Yes, quite,' she agreed without a flicker of hesitation. 'I am older even than you, never mind than she. So, depending upon the cause of the attack, I am safe … or not.'

He turned away and made no answer.

Amelia, who could not have heard this latter exchange, made a sweeping statement about the Princess of Wales, and Georgiana replied. Conversation moved on.

Soon after, the gentlemen remained at the table for the port to be passed. The ladies excused themselves to the withdrawing room. By mutual agreement, they discussed fashion and other subjects that would usually be anything from harmless and graceful to downright vicious. Tonight, they were all content with the former.

When the gentlemen rejoined them three-quarters of an hour later, Narraway was not with them. Vespasia made no comment.

As soon as the port was passed, Narraway declined, claiming the wine was too heavy for him after such a splendid meal, and excused himself. There was no way he could leave discreetly: with only four of them, he would be missed, regardless of anything he said. By now, it was fully dark outside, except for the half-moon, when the ragged clouds parted. It was his one chance to re-hide the package where no one would find it. And he had to assume they would look.

He went straight to the garden room and changed into a pair of rubber boots that he knew were left there for the convenience of guests. He took one of the heavier coats off the pegs and stepped outside. The air hit him like an icy slap across the face, the wind sharp behind it. He was tempted to step back inside, but he must put the package which, at the moment, was in his inside jacket pocket, somewhere where it would not be found.

He walked along the gravel pathway around the corner of the wing, and then down beside the first big herbaceous border. The wind was in his face. He knew exactly where he was going, and he had a small torch in his pocket to define the precise spot when he arrived.

A winding river ran through the land. Part of it curved into the garden, and then out again. The part where it ran through the estate was a hundred yards long, or so, and made a large pool before it hung over a steep weir, the current twisting, turning, eddying back on itself before continuing on, and eventually below the weir sweeping back across the fields again. There was a slender bridge over it, just above the actual fall, which was four or five feet high, a significant drop. The pool above it held lilies and was an excellent place for fish, were fishing permitted. Narraway had a place in mind that he had noticed the previous time he had walked in this direction. It was a hole in the crossbeams of the woodwork supporting the bridge, only visible from one angle, and deep enough to reach a whole arm into, and hide something from sight.

He walked steadily, with his head down against the biting cold. Perhaps they were going to have a white Christmas after all. At this temperature, it would be sleet at first, but if it went on for any length of time, it would be snow. He increased speed a little. He had not left the tell-tale evidence of footprints.

Dinner had been ghastly, and yet he was smiling when he thought of how swiftly Vespasia had come to his defence. It was instinctive, without thought, so different from the usual coolness she projected, the perfect composure. And so unlike her. It was the intensity of emotion that had made him realise that she had defended him because she thought he was vulnerable. So he was, but not to Cavendish's rather silly slight about birth and preferment. He was vulnerable to the real failures. Alone in this bitter night, he was honest. He was vulnerable to loving too much to hide it, to guard against it, to the overwhelming pleasure it brought him, and the fear of losing any part of it. He was vulnerable to not living up to what she thought of him, to the respect he would lose if she knew how he had failed in Normandy. Not only had it cost Edith her life, when she had trusted him to guard her, but he had never solved the mystery of her death. He had not even known what happened to the package she was to have handed over. It was the only thing in his career from which he had salvaged nothing!

It was beginning to spit, like needles of ice on his cheeks. At least it kept his attention on where he was going. He was nearly at the river. He could hear the roar of the water over the weir. After the earlier rain, the current was strong and deep.

It took him several minutes to find the place and poke the heavily wrapped package inside the hole. Please heaven the river did not rise another foot in the next couple of days!

He turned and walked back quickly. He was shaking with cold, but at least the wind was at his back now, and the smell of the damp earth was pleasant. The knowledge of its beauty was with him, even though he could not see it at this moment.

Vespasia listened to the conversation in the withdrawing room and made all the necessary remarks to appear as if she were paying attention. She was, more or less, but not to the words, more to the intonations, the choice of phrases that sometimes gave away more than was intended. Above all, she watched faces and hands. It was surprising how many women did not know what to do with their hands. Georgiana had ugly, short fingers with large knuckles. She did not wear rings, other than her wedding ring, and she kept her hands concealed in the folds of her skirt. She was well aware that her hair was her best feature, although it was beginning to lose the vibrancy of its autumnal colour. But she had courage. She was luke-warm about very little. She might be misguided at times; she was hardly ever indifferent.

'Tell me why you think so!' Vespasia said suddenly. 'I mean, regarding labour law.'

Georgiana turned and looked at her with surprise. 'Why? So you can tell me why you think I'm wrong?'

'Are you?' Vespasia asked. 'What would I be able to point out so easily? Perhaps *I* am wrong? Listening to you, it occurs to me I have gained my opinions from others, and have not thought about it myself.'

Georgiana regarded her suspiciously, but must have decided to answer anyway. She gave a vivid argument, with examples, of her point of view.

Vespasia listened, and was obliged to agree. It was not an unpleasant experience. It amused her how startled Georgiana was, as if she had bitten into what she had supposed to be a lemon, and found that actually it was sweet.

'You never know, do you?' Rosalind observed. 'People are not always what you think, at all. When you know them a little better …'

'That is the argument for very long engagements,' Amelia answered a trifle too quickly. 'Not that it really helps. *Would* it help to know in advance?'

'Not at all, if you can't get out of it,' Georgiana remarked. 'Family and all that …'

Vespasia knew exactly what she meant. Her own first marriage had been more suitable to her parents than to her. But she had fared better than many.

Amelia was looking at her steadily. 'I imagine if one can survive long enough, with teeth and hair and able to stand upright, a second chance might be made with more freedom, even if not any more sense! I believe Lord Narraway is considerably younger than you are?'

'If you need to ask that, then I am doing very well,' Vespasia replied, torn between laughing and biting back really hard. She chose the former, conscious once more of the pain in Amelia, rather than the spite. She thought of the old saying, 'Too unhappy to be kind', and how apposite it was.

Rosalind looked up. 'I thought you were going to say that the field of choice becomes rather sparse! Actually, sparser than when you were twenty.'

'Everything is sparser than when I was twenty, my dear,' Vespasia told her. 'But some things are also better. And added to that, one learns what is really of value.'

'Indeed,' Rosalind said softly. 'And it is not always what we expected.'

Vespasia did not answer that. Her thoughts sharpened and clarified in her mind. She must face this issue soon, very soon, whatever the truth of it, or even more painful, perhaps, the reasons behind it.

Conversation became general again, and after twenty minutes, the three men joined them.

'I'm sorry,' Cavendish said to Vespasia. 'Narraway took himself off without saying anything, so I have no idea where he went. Possibly to bed, although it's absurdly early. He did not appear to be ill.'

Vespasia took a risk. 'Perhaps he went to see if Iris is improving? She might be regaining consciousness, and then she can tell us what actually happened to her.'

'I thought we knew that,' Rosalind said softly. 'What we don't know is who did it. Or why.'

'Don't we know why?' Vespasia asked.

'I don't know why,' Georgiana complained. 'Most of the thoughts that came to my mind are distinctly

uncharitable. If you can suggest an answer that is …
morally acceptable … I would be happy to hear it.
Maybe we all would.'

'Hardly an affair …' Vespasia followed the thought
she had begun, and could not now gracefully leave.
'In the orangery, in the middle of the night, and more
importantly, in the middle of winter!'

'But that's where we found her!' Amelia protested.
'You can't escape that!'

'Alone,' Vespasia pointed out.

'Are you suggesting she tripped over her own feet
and fell, knocking herself out? Please don't expect
anyone else to credit that.'

'No, of course not. Only that she was not necessarily there for a romantic assignation,' Vespasia said.

'If you don't want to be absurd,' Cavendish interrupted impatiently, 'then face the obvious. The
assignation was with your husband! God knows what
is the matter between a beautiful young woman and
a man at least twice her age.'

'Yes, you've said that before,' she countered. 'An
affair is unlikely. So, what was it then? What did you
have in mind?'

He had not expected that response. He hesitated.

'You had better answer her, Cavendish. It's too late

to argue secrecy now,' Dorian Brent told him wearily. 'Of course she had an assignation. No one goes down to an icy-cold orangery in the middle of the night unless it's for a damn good reason. She met Narraway there, whoever she thought she was going to meet. He left, going outside, so he says. She came back and someone struck her so hard she may still die.' He looked up. 'How is she? Has anyone checked on her recently?'

'We all have,' Rosalind answered. 'At one time or another.'

'That doesn't leave a lot of credible answers.' Brent resumed his argument. 'It means either Cavendish or Allenby was who she expected to see.'

'Or Narraway,' Amelia said quickly. 'With only his word for it that he left the orangery and came back when she was still there. Why should we believe him? Or for that matter, you?'

Vespasia turned and looked at Cavendish, and in that moment saw the triumph in his eyes. This was what he wanted, perhaps what it was about: some revenge upon Narraway. But why? A chill touched her that perhaps Narraway knew, and that was what hurt him so much.

Narraway came in from the hallway just as

Vespasia rose to her feet. 'Good night,' she said to the room in general, then walked towards Narraway, took his arm, and accompanied him back towards the door, and out into the hall. She could feel the cold air coming from him, as if his whole being, from the skin of his face through to the bone, were frozen.

They did not speak all the way up the grand staircase, past the high-carved newels at the top, and over the deep carpeted landing to their bedroom door. As soon as the door was closed behind them, she faced him. 'You are frozen. Do you want to have a hot bath before we speak and … get warm?'

He smiled bleakly. 'It sounds as if your withdrawal after dinner was more than a little tense?'

'Indeed, it was. But I learned a thing or two.'

'From the women?' He looked surprised.

'Of course, from the women.' She controlled her impatience so that it was almost inaudible in her voice. This was the time for wisdom, but not even a shadow of impatience. There was neither time nor emotion to waste. She could see the distress in the lines of his face. Usually they imparted strength, but now they betrayed weariness, and also a new vulnerability. Or at least one she had not recognised

157

before. She decided in that instant to stop sparring, dancing around the subject, trying to introduce it tactfully.

She let out her breath slowly. 'Victor, there is no time for this. I know you came here to take the package from Iris, and then after we have left, to pass it on to whoever is next in line, and eventually to someone it is intended for. You knew that before you came, and she must have known it also. It appears that someone else knew as well. Perhaps that was the intention, too. To repeat a version of an earlier scenario in order to punish you.'

'Vespasia! You can't believe that—'

'I don't.' She cut across him before he could finish the thought. 'What I do believe is that something like this happened once before, in Normandy, a long time ago.'

'More than twenty years.'

'And somehow you failed, or felt that you did.' She took a breath and steadied herself. 'And it involved Max Cavendish.'

'No, I didn't even know him then.' He looked confused. 'The girl in Iris's place was also attacked, but she was killed,' he said softly. 'I never knew who did it. I think it was a man named Philippe. I started making enquiries again later … but I don't know.'

'You may not have known Cavendish, but he is involved somehow,' she pointed out.

'What makes you think that? He had nothing to do with it at all!' Narraway replied.

'Somehow he did,' she insisted. 'It's in his face. It's not as simple as envy of you for money or position, or title. It's personal. What happened, Victor?' she insisted. 'We need to know. We need to be right, if we are to bring this to a just end. What happened? What was your part in it?' She tried to be gentle, to take some part of the pain to herself, but there was no way.

'There were several of us there, like this party. Everything on the surface was fine. A package to be passed over, discreetly at an event that seemed trivial. Rich people enjoying themselves …' He stopped, his face filled with grief.

'Let it go, Victor,' she said very gently.

'I can't. He killed Edith. If you'd known her, you would understand. She was like Iris, young and brave, full of dreams.'

'And you loved her?' she said very gently.

'I hardly knew her.' His voice cracked and he had

to clear his throat to continue. 'But she trusted me to keep her safe, and I failed … completely. I didn't even catch him.'

His face was full of pain, and she believed also of guilt. That was what hurt her. Not that he might have loved someone else twenty years ago. There would be something missing in him if he had never loved before, something essential to sanity, to a whole heart. It was that he carried that guilt with him still, and the anger. Perhaps it was the anger that was the worst. The unforgiving of himself. 'And you have started looking into this Philippe again? Could he have heard that you did?'

'I … suppose so. It's not likely, though.'

How could she tell him that he might never catch Philippe and that he was hurting not Philippe, but himself, by pursuing it still? 'Tell me about it,' she said instead.

He looked away. 'It's over. You're right. They could all of them be dead, for all I know.'

'They're not dead to you, and that is what matters. At least to me it is.'

He looked up at her. 'Why? None of them can change anything now. And it has nothing to do with Cavendish.'

'It is not what happened that matters any more,' she answered, certain of the truth of it in her mind. 'It is what we make of it that matters now, how we see it. It is still weighing far too heavily on you.'

'I made a bad error!' There was desperation in his voice.

'Victor, we all make bad errors.'

'Have you made any errors that cost another person their life?' he asked bitterly. 'Their hearts, maybe. Their imagination of love, almost certainly. But could you have helped that? I think it arrogant to suppose so. People fall in love for all sorts of reasons, often personal, vulnerable, even fleeting. It's your fault only if you led them on, knowing you did not return their emotions. And I have known you for many years now. I never saw you use your beauty or your social position to gratify your vanity, or to entertain yourself at someone else's expense.' He was avoiding the issue. It was not about love or disappointment. But she needed to answer this, or it would be another evasion.

The answer was not easy to find words for. 'I have done more than play in society, Victor. We have had many revolutionary times since then. Also, I haven't been in England all the time. I have meddled in other nations' affairs, not always with the best results. I

161

lost, in many of the causes I espoused, and wondered how I could have been taken in so easily. They're irrelevant now. I knew kings and princes, soldiers and politicians. I used such wit and beauty as I possessed. I would find it hard to justify now. I succeeded sometimes, and sometimes I failed. In either, I could have been wrong.'

'Wasn't it before we met? Do I need to know about it?' he asked with a slight frown. There was urgency in his voice.

Was he vulnerable to jealousy, for so long ago? It was all in the past now, but she found his emotion touching, possibly ridiculous, but she wanted to ease it all the same. It moved her deeply that it could still matter to him. 'Not at all,' she said easily. 'I thought of it only because you reminded me how simple it is to make mistakes, and allow them to haunt you. Now tell me what happened in Normandy that might have relevance to this. And for heaven's sake, sit down, even if you would prefer to do so on the far side of the bed.'

He walked round and sat on the far side, as she had suggested, but properly on the bed, with his feet up and his head on the piled-up pillows, not looking as if he were wanting to escape.

'It was about twenty years ago,' he began. 'And summer, not Christmas. A beautiful château in the countryside, near the sea. I remember the grasses were almost waist-high, and there were wild flowers. Edith was to hand over a package of documents. I can't quite remember what it was. Letters, I think. Incriminating letters. There were several other guests, to make up the numbers. I appeared to be just one of them, in fact, to watch Edith and keep her safe. Which I failed to do.' He was staring at the far wall, as if he could see the fields of France as he spoke, even smell the wind off the grass and beyond it the sea.

Vespasia knew France as well. It woke the same ache of loveliness in her as it seemed to in him, and some of the same shadows as well. She had regrets, too, but this time her regret was about him. 'What happened?' she asked.

Reluctantly he spoke about the part he had clearly been dreading. 'Edith was dead. I never found the package. Presumably the person who killed her took it.' His voice dropped a tone. 'It never reached its destination, I know that. It's an open wound. It could have been any of them. Just like with Iris. But I heard some news lately, quite by chance, that made me think it was Philippe.'

163

'This is not finished yet,' she interrupted him. 'Iris is not dead. She may recover. And we have the package, and you will deliver it to whom it was intended.' She took a breath. 'But it is Max who wishes to destroy you. He hates you, of that I am perfectly certain.'

He looked at her, eyes narrowed, waiting. 'Quite a few people dislike me, Vespasia.'

'I'm not talking about dislike. If you stand for anything at all, there will be people who dislike you,' she said impatiently. 'I chose the word *hate* because I meant it. I saw it in his face, quite undisguised. He is getting ready for the *coup de grâce*. I ... I think it has nothing to do with Iris. She is incidental.'

'Edith?' he said in disbelief.

'My dear, she is relevant to you because you blame yourself for her death, and perhaps you were at fault. I don't know ...'

He winced.

She felt the pain of it, as if it had wounded her, too. 'What is it? That you are imperfect, too? Like the rest of us? Victor, did you suppose I did not know there were errors, mistakes, and perhaps worse? If not, what would we have in common? You might forgive my flaws, but you would never

164

understand them. There would always be blemishes you would prefer were not there. Unlooked-for scars? Can you really forgive, if you have no need to be forgiven?'

He stopped even trying to hide the doubt, and the need in him. 'Have you scars … like that?'

'You ask as if you thought I were perfect,' she said, smothering her own sharp knowledge of fault.

'Is that what makes you so beautiful? Mercy?' he said softly.

Suddenly her eyes filled with tears and she reached forward to put her lips to his cheek. 'Oh, for heaven's sake, don't be so … absurd. I love you! I wouldn't if you were perfect, and invulnerable! It's a journey. You are not there yet, and neither am I!'

He turned a little to touch his lips to hers, and then kissed her long, gently, and more deeply, and then again, this time on her neck, and gently pulled away the lace covering her bosom, and she put out her arms to draw him closer.

The following day was Christmas Eve. It had rained in the night and then the wind had blown the cloud away and daylight brought spectacular sun on films of ice. Every bare branch or twig was crusted with

165

it, every blade of the sparse winter grass was shivering with crystals.

'I think today we shall finish it,' was all Vespasia said before they went down to breakfast. She did not mention Cavendish's hatred again. 'We must do something to precipitate the final action. Because if we don't, he will! And he is too clever for us to allow him that advantage.'

'I'm quite aware of that,' Narraway said with a tight smile. 'As is poor James.'

'He doesn't know it is Cavendish!' she reminded him. 'And I am certainly not going to keep an appointment with anyone in the orangery, at midnight or any other time.'

'I hope you're not. Besides, I don't imagine he would be so obliging as to repeat himself. If indeed it is he. And we have not proved that.'

'I don't believe it is Rafe Allenby,' she said. 'And it is Dorian Brent's job here to protect her. It would be self-defeating to his career, as well as pointless, to have attacked her. I've been thinking about something I saw in the garden the day after we arrived. I'd almost forgotten about it but it came back to me when I first woke and now I understand. I saw James and Dorian Brent quarrelling in the garden.

They even came to blows. James accused Dorian of following Iris about, but now I know how these things work – now that you've explained the courier has a protector – I realise that's Dorian's role. He evaded a proper explanation to James, and that makes sense, too. His look of blank despair now and again must be because he feels as you did in Normandy.'

'Yes, you must be right. If only I'd seen for them for myself I might have guessed then. But you couldn't possibly interpret what you saw, and doubtless thought Dorian was just making a fool of himself.'

'That leaves only Cavendish, or some stranger who broke into the orangery in the night. We have already dismissed that as absurd. Cavendish must feel the net closing around him. He cannot imagine you will let it go! He has some knowledge of Normandy. He must have! Who is Philippe to him? Who is anyone who was there?'

'I don't know …' He stopped.

'Know what? What is it, Victor?'

'I was going to say he had no connection with the Home Office then, and so nothing to do with Special Branch, but I forgot that he did … very briefly …

and disastrously for his career. It was before he married Amelia. He was totally unsuited to the position, and that cost him a safe seat in Parliament.'

'And you were responsible?'

'No. It was his own damn fault! But I was the one who eventually tripped him up. I could have let it slide, but I was a bit more judgemental then.'

'Was your judgement wrong?' she asked perfectly levelly.

'If he's behind this, then I was right. And don't say I pushed him into it. The position needed a man who could not be persuaded to act against his nature, by me, or anyone else. But he wanted it. He was ambitious. It still scalds him that Amelia had the money and the title. Not that it makes any difference now, except to the balance between them. History will repeat itself; they have only daughters.'

'So, it will not be Cavendish Hall any more,' she said.

'Did you know her before she married him?' he asked with some surprise.

'When we first met it must have been just after Genevieve died.'

'Genevieve?'

'His first wife. She was very sweet. Or perhaps I remember her that way because she died so young ... in childbirth.'

'I could forgive Cavendish a lot for that,' he said quietly.

'It happens. Women do die in childbirth ... it is not rare.'

'And the child, too?' His voice betrayed his imagination of the pain.

'I think her parents took him. Wait, I don't think it was a boy. No, I'm almost certain it was a girl,' she corrected herself.

'So, Cavendish lost her, too,' Narraway said quietly.

Vespasia shook her head. 'I don't know. I've never heard him mention her. Certainly, Amelia's never had her. After breakfast, I think I'll go for a brief walk. It's a wonderful garden, the one thing in all this that is totally unspoiled.'

'Well, you'd better enjoy it while you can, my dear,' he said wryly. 'Because I am perfectly certain we will not be invited again.'

They set off down the wide sweeping staircase and across the hall to the dining room where breakfast was set out. All of the others, except James, were there and had begun their meal.

'You look a little pale, Vespasia,' Amelia observed. 'I hope you are quite well. Is it all … too much for you?' It was said quite gently, but no one missed the barb beneath it.

Vespasia gave a secret little smile. On the face of a woman less beautiful it might have been called a smirk. 'There are things for which one never grows too old,' she answered. 'I am glad you provide such a wonderful breakfast. I find I'm quite hungry.' And she went to the sideboard and helped herself to bacon, scrambled eggs, and two slices of fresh crisp toast.

Conversation staggered a bit and then resumed.

'It's a glorious morning,' Rosalind said cheerfully.

'Indeed,' Cavendish agreed. 'But I would take advantage while you can. It is forecast to rain later. Quite heavily, they say.'

Amelia's eyebrows rose. 'Who are *they*?'

'One of the gardening boys, if you need to be precise. Gardeners seem to be a step ahead of us, regarding the weather.' He looked back at the rest of the table and spoke to no one in particular. 'It's rained quite hard in the hills, and the rivers were high anyway. Damn cold last night, but it's going to warm up. No snow for Christmas, I'm afraid, just a couple of feet more water in the river.' He smiled, as if at a memory. 'It's quite dramatic in full flood. Makes quite a whirlpool under the weir. Would you pass me the marmalade, Narraway? It's rather good. Another month or so and it'll be time for a new batch.'

'Oranges … in January?' Georgiana asked in surprise.

'Seville, you know? The only ones that make decent marmalade. Got to have a bite to it or it's not worth bothering.'

No one replied.

Vespasia began her breakfast. She was truly hungry. She had said so to annoy Amelia, but it was not an exaggeration. She had slept well, when they had finally gone to sleep. The things that mattered most in her life were well. In fact, they were very well. There had been a tenderness between them, the depth of which was new, and infinitely sweet.

As soon as she had finished her breakfast, Vespasia excused herself and went to the servants' quarters, specifically the housekeeper's bedroom. It took a moment or two to obtain permission to go inside, an inconvenience she appreciated, and she thanked the footman at the door for his diligence.

Inside, the room was warm, a small fire smouldering in the hearth, and there were coloured candles lit on the mantelpiece and wreaths of bright berried holly on top of the chest of drawers and on the inside of the door, and scarlet ribbons tied to the footposts of the bed.

James was slumped forward in his chair, sound asleep, one hand on the coverlet where he had almost certainly been touching Iris, whose hand lay an inch or two away.

Vespasia closed the door quietly, making only the slightest sound.

Iris moved, very slightly, then she opened her eyes.

Vespasia felt such an upsurge of pleasure her breath caught in her throat. 'Iris? How are you? Can you move?'

'Of course I can move,' Iris said with surprise, and made to sit up. Then she winced and lay back again. 'Oh! My head … hurts. What happened?' Confusion showed in her face, but she made no more effort to move.

Vespasia sat down on the edge of the bed and took Iris's hand, and as Iris's fingers closed over hers she squeezed them very gently. 'Someone hit you when you were in the orangery. I'm afraid you have been unconscious for a couple of days, and we were very afraid for you. But you are obviously going to be fine.'

Iris frowned. 'I don't remember ...' She turned very slowly and looked at James.

'He's been here all the time,' Vespasia told her.

Iris smiled and the tears slid down her cheeks, but they were tears of happiness. 'He wouldn't leave me,' she whispered. 'Ever ...'

'You don't, when you love someone,' Vespasia replied. 'In a minute I shall waken him so he can see you are back again with us. First, I must ask you, do you know who struck you?'

'No ... I ... really don't remember. Maybe it will come back to me...' Iris looked confused again, even guilty.

'No matter.' Vespasia dismissed it with a flick of her hand. 'You are quite safe here in the house-keeper's room, and we will find out.' She stood up and put her hand on James's where it lay on the edge of the bed. She tightened her grip. 'James! Iris is back. I think you should welcome her ...'

James opened his eyes, blinking, trying to remember where he was. Then he saw Iris, still resting against the pillows, but with her eyes open, and smiling at him.

'Iris!' He closed his eyes tightly, then opened them. 'Thank God,' he whispered. 'Thank God!' He reached forward and laid his hand over hers, gazing at her face as if unable to look away in case it was a dream, and the slightest thing would awaken him.

'I imagine you might like a cup of tea,' Vespasia interrupted him. 'Shall I ask the housekeeper to send in a tray?'

James looked up at her. 'Yes, please.'

Vespasia went out of the door, smiling, told the footman to remain where he was, and went to look for Mrs Pugh.

The housekeeper was delighted, but Vespasia instructed her to say nothing to the rest of the staff yet.

'It was not an accident, Mrs Pugh,' she said quietly. 'Somebody did this, and may well try again, if we are not careful. Please leave the guard at the door, and do not yet spread the good news.'

'Very well, m'lady, but I'm ever so pleased she's

come to. And her husband, poor man. I don't think he's eaten a thing! Who would have done it? Couldn't it have been an accident?'

'I'm afraid not. But we will find out, and it will be taken care of. But for the time being, silence is the safest thing for us all.'

She told Narraway when she found him alone in the magnificent library. It was a room that at another time she would have been happy to spend a whole day in, or even two. He was sitting in one of the deep green leather chairs. He looked up immediately on hearing her footsteps.

She closed the door behind her. 'Iris is awake,' she said, almost under her breath.

'Thank God! Who have you told?' he asked.

'Mrs Pugh, the housekeeper, whom I've instructed to keep quiet. The danger's not past; she doesn't remember anything …'

'Too early to say whether she ever will,' he answered immediately.

'I'll stay with her,' Vespasia promised. 'If I have to go, I'll make sure at least two of the servants are around. And I doubt James will leave, except for a change of clothes.'

He nodded briefly. No more was necessary. They understood each other completely.

It was a long, strange day. The tension did not ease. As far as anyone else knew, Iris was still unconscious, and someone still in this house had attacked her, presumably with the intent to kill. Vespasia was in and out of the housekeeper's room. Mrs Pugh saw to it that Iris had clean linen, and clean clothes to wear as soon as she would be recovered enough and it was safe to let her survival be known.

Narraway, too, was renewed in the best way. Old ghosts had still to be laid to rest, but they no longer frightened him. The pain was that of wounds healing, not of the new loss that he had feared.

He knew that Cavendish was telling him about the river because he suspected that he had hidden the package there. He must have seen how cold Narraway was when he'd returned from hiding the package, and noted how long he'd been gone, then made a very good guess. He was taunting him, seeing if he would take the bait. If he'd guessed wrongly he would no doubt set his bait in another way. But if Cavendish were speaking the truth, and the river rose even one foot, the package would be ruined, whether it was retrievable or not.

And perhaps it was a good thing to provoke a confrontation. At least he would deny Cavendish the advantage of complete surprise, though of course he would know every yard of his garden, and Narraway had only a rough idea of it.

The afternoon drew towards a close. Vespasia and Narraway had changed for dinner and were still in the bedroom, preparing to go down.

'I have to go …' he said.

'I know,' she agreed quickly. 'It's dangerous, but worse to leave it.'

'You have to stay here. He knows what …'

'I'll not allow myself to be alone,' she interrupted. 'Better than that, I'll stay with Dorian Brent. We've agreed he plays in this the role you played in Normandy.'

'Not a high recommendation,' he said sadly.

She felt the guilt rather than heard it. 'Would you prefer that I stay with Iris? Then James will be there, and possibly a footman.'

'Yes, do. Then at least two of you will be safe. He will follow me …' he pointed out.

'Don't tell me comfortable lies, Victor. He could

wait until you return, and then hold you hostage to hand the package over in exchange for Iris's life, or more …'

'I don't think so. That would make it impossible to deny his part in it, and that leaves very little room for negotiation …' he argued.

'But if you know, then it's finished for him anyway.'

He met her soft, silver-grey eyes and knew he had explained too much. 'I will be the one who comes back. Or escapes. As you reminded me, this is not a copy of the Normandy case. There is not much similarity, except the passing of the information discreetly, and my presence. I'm looking for reflections that aren't there, and Cavendish knows nothing about that.'

'But he smells blood in the water all the same,' she said. 'Be careful.' It took all her nerve to say that steadily, as if he were doing no more than going for a walk in the fresh air. She forced out of her imagination's grasp that this might be goodbye. In life that was always possible. More so as the years added up. Never take a moment lightly.

She walked over to him and put her arms around him. He was quick to respond. He kissed her face, her brow, her cheek, her mouth. Then he turned and walked out of the bedroom without saying anything more, not even telling her again to be careful. All the words had been said.

He went across the landing and down the long, sweeping staircase into the hall, across the marble flagstones and into the passage to the garden room. It was the obvious place to go outside because the coats and boots were there. If Cavendish were watching him, or requesting a servant to do so, he would see him, whichever door he used. And, of course, there was always the possibility that Cavendish had gone ahead of him. There was more than one way to approach the weir and the bridge, but in the end there was only a single path that finished beside the bank. Cavendish could be anywhere along the way.

Narraway fastened his coat and stepped outside. Cavendish had been right. It was warmer. The evening storm, already rattling and whining through the bare branches of the trees, was going to be rain, not snow. There would be no snow clinging to the branches further upstream; it had all run off into the river.

He walked swiftly, turning from side to side often to see any approaching figure, any extra density to a bush that could conceal a man behind it. He reached the arch of the pergola, the twisted stems of the climbing roses wound through its arches and cross-beams. In summer, they would all be hidden by leaves, and for the last few months in June and July, smothered with a foam of white roses.

The walks on the other side were empty, as far as he could see in a torch's gleam. He did not want to use it: it made him visible from a hundred feet away. But to be without it, once a cloud swallowed light like this, was to invite not only getting lost, but falling over a broken branch, or even a heavy stone misplaced, a brick out of a walkway, or one of the low walls.

His shoulders were tight, his whole body locked almost rigid. His sense told him that Cavendish would not attack him until he had possession of the package. Whatever he planned, Narraway had to have it with him.

A gust of wind blew the increasingly heavy rain into his face, and a few last wet leaves. It was impossible to tell if the sounds were branches thrashing, small animals, such as rabbits or even foxes, darting through the undergrowth, or a human being treading softly, moving alongside him, invisible in the darkness.

What did Cavendish intend to do? What was his plan, beyond getting this package from Narraway? Had this been his plan all the way through, from the first invitation to come for Christmas? Or had he changed it as events transpired? What was the purpose? Was it about the package? Getting it to the right people ... or the wrong people? For that matter, did Cavendish know it had been doctored or not?

Or had it been about getting revenge on Narraway all along? And the package was incidental. No more than a suitable means.

He came to the end of the walkway, climbed the shallow steps, and turned along the avenue of beech trees. Their bare trunks gleamed wet in the faint light, really only a paler darkness.

Was Cavendish's hatred of Narraway so deep that destroying him, his work, his life, his reputation, was all that he really needed?

Narraway must put it out of his mind. It did not matter. Only survival mattered now!

Was Cavendish going to come after him, here along the river bank? Narraway was safe until Cavendish could catch him with the package. His death was not enough. If Vespasia was correct, Cavendish wanted to ruin him as well. Then Narraway would not be able to explain anything. Once Cavendish took the package from him, he had simply to slip on the river bank and fall into the flooding water, perhaps below the weir, where the current swirled white and sucked under and burst out again twenty yards down the river, wide and deep. Cavendish could say he tried to save him, but it was his own life or Narraway's. Who was to argue with him?

It was definitely the water he could hear now. That wasn't rain beating on the leaves. There were no leaves left; they were all a pale carpet on the ground. He was in an open space, but sheltered from the wind that was thrashing the saplings on the far side. The footbridge across the river creaked; the water tipping over the edge of the weir gleamed white.

Narraway turned slowly, searching the bank, first the near side, then the far. He could see nothing but the grass, and here and there a low bush of gorse.

Was he imagining it that Cavendish would follow him? Perhaps he would wait and attack him when he came back to the house? Red-handed, as it were? With the plans in his pocket.

No. That was far too risky. Cavendish could

simply hide them somewhere else in this huge garden. If he did not have them, then there was nothing to tie them to him. He would come back into the house, and there would be nothing to defend, to explain.

Narraway was standing on the grass facing the bank and it was bitterly cold. The wind was rising and it was beginning to rain harder. Whether Cavendish was here or not, Narraway needed to get the package. Perhaps Cavendish was too clever to take the bait, and this was a double bluff. Maybe he would blame it all on Narraway? Say he had attacked Iris and stolen the package to give to someone quite different from whomever the Home Office had intended. If Iris had no memory of what had happened to her in the orangery, or if Cavendish still found a way to kill him, then Narraway had no proof of his own innocence.

Narraway walked across the open grass and down the bank, towards the place where he had hidden the package, within the struts of the bridge. Water was foaming almost to his feet. It had risen twelve inches since he and Vespasia had arrived. It was now fast and deep, and it would get deeper. He balanced very carefully. The ground was soggy, likely to give way beneath his weight. He felt for the hole. Extraordinary how loath he was to put his bare hand into the space he could not see. What if an animal had found shelter there? An animal with a strong jaw and razor teeth?

Don't be so damned stupid! Get the package! He felt for it, and his finger closed on emptiness. He had not reached in far enough. His feet were sinking into the wet grass, below which the actual river mud was deep. He reached up with the other hand to hang on to the wooden struts. It was a ridiculous position, impossibly precarious. Why the hell was he doing this at his age? Because he wanted to be useful one last time! It was supposed to have been easy. And there was pride in it – at least, there had been. He wanted to prove that he could do it, and lay the ghost of Edith and Normandy to rest.

He felt something, inched a little further, and caught the end of the wrapping. He got it between his fingers, then pulled at it until he could get his finger and thumb to it. It would serve him right if water rats had unwrapped it to use it for nesting. Water rats! Urgh!

He pulled at it hard and almost lost it. He was sweating with relief under his heavy jacket, when he heard the voice above him, on the bridge across the weir.

'Excellent! Afraid there might have been something nasty in there? We get eels in the river, occasionally, and they have a hell of a bite, you know!' It was Cavendish, of course.

Narraway could feel his feet sliding in the mud. He was actually standing in the river, ice cold and already up to his ankles. He could not get a purchase to reach up and catch hold of the wood of the bridge.

'Inconsiderate of you,' Cavendish went on. 'How the hell are you going to explain to Vespasia what you were doing messing around in the water this time of night? It's ridiculous. Here! Let me give you a hand.' He reached down with both his arms.

'If you didn't know what I was doing, why are you here?' Narraway said a little breathlessly, trying to grasp a spar of wood just above him. The water was stronger than he had expected, and growing deeper by the second as he slid further into the mud.

'Followed you, old chap. Knew you'd have to come and get your precious package, before the river took it.'

Narraway had no hold on the bridge now. The

current was over his knees and it was like liquid ice. He could not keep his footing much longer.

Cavendish laughed. It was an eerie, detached sound in the wind.

Narraway used all his strength to pull on both of Cavendish's hands and Cavendish could not resist the weight. He was already leaning too far over the bridge to right himself. 'Stop it, you damn fool!' he yelled. 'You'll drown us both!' He heaved at Narraway, trying now to pull him up again.

Narraway completely lost his footing and was a dead weight, in the water right up to his waist. He could not stay conscious much longer, and he knew it. The cold would take him even before he drowned.

'Why?' Narraway gasped. 'It's a false one ... to mislead them!'

'It's not the package, you fool!' Cavendish said between his teeth. 'I don't give a damn what happens to it! It's you! I want you to know you didn't save Iris – just as you didn't save Edith! You're a failure, an arrogant, stupid failure ...' His voice broke and became a sob.

Narraway was frozen and the river was growing deeper. His feet were losing traction in the mud and he was still slipping. But slowly in his mind it was making sense. Edith ... How did Cavendish know about her?

'Philippe killed Edith,' Narraway said between clenched teeth. It was a guess. He did not know, but he believed it. He was so cold and he was sinking further with the water.

'I know!' Cavendish pulled him up a bit. 'And you let him! It was your job to look after her!'

'How do you know? You weren't ...' His mind was becoming clouded with the cold penetrating his whole body.

'Special Branch?' Cavendish's face seemed to be closer. He was hanging on to Narraway, determined now that he should know everything. 'No, I wasn't. Edith was my daughter – all I had left of my Genevieve. She trusted you, and you let her die! Philippe told me all about it. He knew, because he killed her! He boasted about it!'

'Philippe ... I'll ...' Narraway wanted to say something about catching him, but he was going to die. Cavendish had only to let go of him; it was as easy as that.

'You'll what? Kill him? You haven't the guts. And as usual, you're too late. I've taken care of that. Now it's your turn.'

187

With the last ounce of strength he had, Narraway leaned back, managed to brace his feet against the upright of the bridge, and pulled hard. The frail structure gave way, its guardrails smashed by Cavendish's weight. There was a tremendous splash as he fell, pulling one of the rails with him, closer to the middle of the stream. Narraway watched him struggle, flailing in the air for long seconds, and then he was carried over the edge of the weir and disappeared into the white, swirling cauldron of the pool below.

Narraway was paralysed with horror and, for an instant, even more with regret. With blinding clarity, it all made sense. Perhaps there was even justice in it. Iris for Edith.

He was so cold he could not feel his body. Was this what death was like? A slowly growing cold until you felt nothing at all, and then darkness?

Except that he could see lights, dancing lights.

And then there was shouting.

More lights along the bank. A hand on him, grasping, pulling.

Dorian Brent was shouting at him, but his words made no sense.

For a little while all was darkness, then he opened

188

his eyes and there was brandy in his mouth. He swallowed it. Lantern light swayed above him.

'All right! Pick him up. Gently! Don't want to break his arms and legs now. Or drop him!' Brent's voice again. They had come for him. Vespasia!

He thought he saw her beautiful, anxious face and he spoke her name, but the word was only in his head.

They carried him up to the house, and by the time he was there he was fully conscious.

'I'm all right,' he insisted. 'Cavendish? Did you get him too?'

'I'm sorry,' Brent answered. 'He went over the weir and there was no chance. Have some more brandy.' The tone made it plain it was an order.

'What time is it?' Narraway asked.

'About eight o'clock. Why?'

'I want to go home for Christmas ...'

'A bit late for that ...'

'I don't care.' Narraway struggled to get up. 'We can still be there by midnight. It's only a couple of hours. Less, this late. No traffic. Have someone pack my things ... please. Please, Brent. I'll take a hot bath, and put on some dry clothes, and I'll be all right.'

'I'll ask Lady Vespasia …'

'You will do as I ask you! Help me up!'

'As I said, I'll ask Lady Vespasia.'

When they dragged Narraway out of the water, all Vespasia could think of was her overwhelming relief. He was alive. It was all that mattered. They would treat him, look after him. He would be back to himself, in time.

Then, as they carried him back to the house, she realised that Cavendish was gone. He could not have survived going over the falls in that bitter water. In fact, Narraway had been rescued only just in time. Another few minutes and the cold would have stopped his heart and the water filled his lungs. The thought choked her and tears filled her eyes.

There was no need for explanations. It was clear now that Cavendish had been behind it all. There was time for the other answers later. Now, Amelia must be devastated, as numb with shock and grief as any river coldness could make her. Whether she had loved Cavendish or not was irrelevant. And whether she and Vespasia were enemies, rivals or friends was also beside the point. As she walked up the dark path, slowly, feeling her way, as they all were, she wondered how much Amelia knew. Some of the story could be pieced together by the fact that it was Cavendish who had followed Narraway to the river. Would anyone deny that? Surely, he must be the one who had tried to kill Iris?

The lights of the house were ahead. They went the last few yards before the butler met them and guided them in to where Mrs Pugh was waiting with hot water, brandy, and blankets.

Narraway was conscious, just. Vespasia waited only long enough to be certain he knew she was close, and then she went to do what she knew she must.

Amelia was standing alone in the hall, dazed and ashen. She was not aware of Vespasia until Vespasia stood beside her. She turned with fear in her face.

'It is all being taken care of,' Vespasia said quietly. 'Come and sit down. The fire will still be good enough in the drawing room. Someone will bring us a cup of tea. It will warm you and give you strength.'

Amelia stood perfectly still.

Vespasia took her arm and steered her towards the withdrawing room. She was aware of a maid standing helplessly. 'Tea, please,' she told the girl. 'Hot and strong. And bring sugar, or honey. Don't forget it. Now go.'

The girl turned wordlessly and obeyed.

Vespasia took Amelia into the withdrawing room and made her sit down while she poked the fire herself, and put a few more pieces of coal on it. Then she sat down opposite Amelia, took a deep breath, and began. 'I'm so sorry …'

Amelia blinked, then looked at Vespasia as if focusing on her for the first time. 'Sorry? Are you?'

'Yes, of course I am. You have lost your husband in the most distressing circumstances. Whether this is a shock to you, or you knew, or guessed much of it, it is still a terrible blow.'

Amelia glared at her. She seemed for a few moments to be on the edge of denying it, of fighting back. Then her eyes filled with tears and she bent her head and wept.

Vespasia waited a moment or two, uncertain, then followed her own feelings and took Amelia in her arms and held her, very gently. Had Amelia known all about Cavendish, or feared something like it? Or had she been blind to it until today?

The maid brought in the tea and, at a nod from Vespasia, left again.

Vespasia poured two cups and put honey in them both. She waited a few moments for it to cool, then spoke.

'Amelia, take a sip of tea. It will help. You have much to face, but you will not have to do it alone.'

Slowly, Amelia brushed her windblown hair off her face and blinked several times. Her handkerchief was wet with tears already, but she wiped her eyes with it.

'How long have you known?' she asked.

'Not until tonight,' Vespasia answered.

'That's not like you,' Amelia said with a bleak half-smile.

Vespasia hunted for words that would not add to the pain. There was more than enough of that already. 'You will miss him.'

'Yes. It is … shock … but I will be all right!' Amelia said it with a surge of resolve, as if she had suddenly realised she could make it true.

'Of course you will,' Vespasia agreed.

'I … thank you.' Amelia was suddenly awkward.

Vespasia smiled. 'Not at all.'

A few minutes later she met Georgiana in the hall. She did not say anything; an exchange of glances was sufficient. She, too, was ill at ease. She must have realised Dorian's role, or perhaps he had even had the sense to tell her.

'Go back to Lord Narraway,' Georgiana said. 'I will stay with Amelia.'

Vespasia did not demur when asked about leaving that night. Cavendish Hall was now a place of mourning, and in the circumstances their presence would not help. In fact, it might only add shame and embarrassment to the grief that could not be avoided. Cavendish had died attempting to kill Victor, for a reason many would understand, possibly even forgive, but too much else was changed and it was Cavendish who had lost.

Vespasia sat beside Narraway in the hastily harnessed carriage, and footmen were called to assist. Cases were repacked and stowed on the back. The night was very dark, but their own carriage lamps were sufficient, and soon they came to the outskirts of the city, where the roads were lit.

'I'm sorry,' Narraway said gently. 'This is not what Christmas is meant to be. We'll have no goose, no Christmas pudding, no red candles or a decorated tree.'

Vespasia took his hand between hers. 'That is not

what Christmas is meant to be. It's nice, but it's not important.'

'Isn't it?'

'Not in the least. In fact, it sometimes gets in the way. Christmas is about accepting that we all make mistakes, for which we will be forgiven, but first we must forgive others, and then when the knot slips undone and lets go, we can forgive ourselves as well.'

The carriage stopped and Vespasia wound down the misted window and saw they were home. She could hear church bells filling the air with music.

It was Christmas Day.